# VALERIE'S ELITES

## VALERIE'S ELITES, BOOK 1

JUSTIN SLOAN     PT HYLTON     MICHAEL ANDERLE

*To Ugulay, Verona and Brendan Sloan*
*—Justin*

*To Kim*
*—P.T.*

*To Family, Friends and*
*Those Who Love*
*To Read.*
*May We All Enjoy Grace*
*To Live the Life We Are*
*Called.*
*—Michael*

## Space: The *Singlaxian Grandeur*

The *Singlaxian Grandeur* touched down on the first planet in the Vurugu system, an uncharted habitable sector at the edge of the known universe. All atmospheric tests were nominal, and with only the slightest trepidation Valerie hit the button to open the ship's doors.

Her first breath of air on this planet brought back memories of the mountains around the fjords back on Earth—cleaner than anything she had experienced until that point, and this had it beat. It carried an interesting scent, like cinnamon.

Not that she was from the fjords. No, she had been born in Old France, before moving to what had once been America and helping to reestablish New York. She had worked hard to bring peace to her corner of Earth, and now the universe called to her.

This was the first planet she had been on out here, her first step toward accomplishing her mission for the Etheric

Federation. The legendary vampire Michael had made her a Justice Enforcer on Earth, one of his own, and when the time came he had asked her to join Colonel Terry Henry Walton and Bad Company. Her first assignment was to take a small team to this system and collect intel, the ultimate goal being to ensure that the inhabitants of this system joined the Etheric Federation in its war against any race that would see the people of Earth or other innocent races harmed.

They had landed in a secluded area under the cover of trees unlike anything she had ever seen. In a sense the leaves reminded her of umbrellas, spreading in every direction from upturned branches covered in blood-red bark. Since the leaves dripped a sap-like substance she decided to call this the "Bleeding Woods," an all-too-appropriate name for the landing spot of two former vampires and their team.

Former vampires, in her mind, because it was hard to think of them as such anymore. There was a time when both Valerie and Robin would have avoided the sun and drunk blood to stay energized, but such requirements had vanished. Michael had changed Valerie with his blood, and Robin had been given fancy Etheric Federation Pod-doc upgrades.

When Valerie stepped onto the alien soil she couldn't help but feel overwhelmed. Her whole life had been spent on Earth, but she'd left it behind to join the fight. To ensure Earth was safe.

Only problem was, she didn't know where to start. They had the intel file Colonel Walton had given her and she could call him whenever she wanted—in theory—but that wasn't exactly her style. She didn't want to be the one who started the first mission of her new job by calling the boss to ask for direction.

Valerie resolved to get this done on her own. Her team may not have had fancy Jean Duke Specials, and their ship may not have been the most advanced in the Etheric Federation, but the team had grit. And with the types of jobs they'd be tackling, grit was the most important thing.

"Is it safe?" A head popped out of the doorway, a man with a flat nose and beady eyes. Bob. She still wasn't sure what to think about him. "I mean, for us…non-vampires."

"I've explained this. I'm not technically a—"

"Yeah, yeah, not really a vampire. Except that you *have* drunk blood using your fangs before to sustain your life-force, correct? And you weren't able to go into the sun."

"Shut up," she replied, turning again to analyze their surroundings. She heard a shuffling noise among the trees.

"I'm just saying… Once a vampire, always a vampire, right?" He stepped through the door and joined Valerie, Robin following close behind.

She severely wanted to punch Bob right now, but he'd been modified in the Pod-doc too. While on Earth only vampires and Weres could use the power she now understood to be Etheric energy, but up here she had to get used to other people being enhanced.

If she punched him it probably wouldn't hurt nearly as much as she would want it to, so she opted to ignore the man. It was her fault, after all—his being here. He had been released from his service as the Pod technician on the other ship, so when Valerie picked her team—dubbed "Valerie's Elites"—she figured she'd give him a second chance. The idea made sense if she ignored what a dick he was, focusing instead on his technical knowhow.

But he was still talking, even though she kept ignoring him.

That was the problem with dicks. They keep pounding relentlessly away. Would he ever give up? Finally she turned and *pushed* fear, one of the talents she possessed but he lacked. It was enough to make his eyes go wide and his jaw clench shut.

Not enough to make him shit himself, though she would have to consider that next time. This, along with being able to read emotions like an aura, separated her from the rest of them. Even Robin, who had received many modifications, didn't have any abilities like that yet.

The timing was perfect too, because the shuffling in the trees came again, along with a stronger scent of incense as red dust flew past. Her best guess was it came from the trees, and could be rubbed off.

She held up a hand for the others to stay put and be quiet. A yelp came from the direction where she guessed her enemy was—if it was an enemy.

Valerie crouched as she ran, then unslung her rifle and knelt next to one of the thicker trees. Instantly a puff of grey spores flew up around her, and she cursed under her breath. It was too late—whatever had made the noise spotted her and charged.

It appeared at first to be a rhino, but then she saw it was a large bipedal figure covered in thick slabs of rock.

She braced herself, and as it collided she rolled back and kicked upward, sending it over her shoulder. Normally that would have sent a full-grown man sailing, but given his weight this male kind of flopped over and landed with a thud.

Two more of them appeared and charged her, and Robin leaped through the air to tackle one. It braced itself, and she hit it with an *oomph* before falling onto her butt.

*Damn.* She knew that Robin was stronger than most vampires—or former vampires. That meant these aliens were tough.

"What are they?" one of the aliens said to another.

"Monsters, or maybe demons," the third said, doing his best to stand but flailing like a turtle.

Valerie and the rest of her team had had a chip implanted that translated most languages, and apparently this one was included.

"More like emissaries," Valerie stated, glad to find her chip translating. "We're not here to fight you."

One of them turned to her with a look of defiance, then positioned himself like a bull about to charge.

She lifted her rifle and aimed at him—it had to be a male with that attitude. "I don't think I made myself clear. We've just arrived, and we're looking for a contest of champions. Perhaps you've heard of it? I'm told it's called the Kost Games."

At the name, the aliens' postures instantly got less aggressive and they looked at her with wide, intrigued eyes.

"Outsiders call it the Kost Games." the lead one said. "Here we call it by its true name. The Damu Michezo. You... You think you can compete in the Damu Michezo?"

Valerie had to laugh. "I'm pretty sure I'll be fine."

The alien cracked his neck, pounded on his stone carapace, and said, "Show me."

"What?"

"You beat me, I'll point you in the right direction. In fact, there was a shuttle headed for the planet it's held on not long ago. You might still be able to catch it, or at least chase it down and follow it. Are you up to it?"

Robin smiled at Valerie, then shrugged and took a step back.

"I don't want to hurt you," Valerie warned. "I mean it."

He scoffed. "I'll tell you a little secret about Qwaza...no one has ever hurt me. You? I won't worry. Come."

Valerie tossed her rifle to Robin, and then her sword. She heard pounding and she turned back to see Qwaza charging damn fast. Valerie had fought her fair share of vampires and Weres on Earth, so she was used to speed. With a quick sidestep, she brought around her leg to sweep him. What she hadn't counted on was his next move, which involved a fast sideways roll to compensate for her new location. He came up like a boulder, unraveling as he regained his footing, and slammed his forehead right into hers.

Red spots filled her vision, and it wasn't only because her eyes had started to glow red. *That fucking hurt!*

When Qwaza next moved, Valerie didn't take any chances. She dodged to the left and tried *pushing* fear, only nothing happened. The alien kept charging forward, and she realized that it wasn't putting off an emotional aura that she could sense—another difference from back home.

He was fast, and apparently immune to her special abilities. That meant she would have to take him down the old-fashioned way, with a straight-up butt-kicking. He plowed into her again, but this time she went with it as her martial arts training back in Old France had taught her. Using her opponent's strength against him, she twisted his arm behind him and slammed him headfirst into the nearest tree. The trunk cracked, dangerously close to snapping in half.

It wasn't like she was trying to kill him, but she also wasn't about to let this guy win—not when her mission depended on it. Without hesitation, she kicked out his leg so that he plowed into the ground head-first.

He growled, trying to spin and get to her, but she was too fast. In the time it took him to maneuver around her she had delivered two knees to his side and then abdomen, an elbow to the temple, and an uppercut to his jaw.

Qwaza stumbled back, looked like he might charge again...and then collapsed onto his butt.

Valerie started to raise her fist in victory, but the alien pulled something sharp from within his carapace—a stone knife. He was up and slashing before Valerie had time to fully process it, and one slash caught her across the cheek. She slammed her forearm into the back of his wrist, knocking the knife from his hand, and then delivered a roundhouse kick so powerful that it cracked Qwaza's carapace and sent him reeling backwards.

"Nobody gets away with that," Qwaza shouted, but his eyes darted to his companions, worry creasing his hard skin. "Get her!"

The others started to move, but Robin stepped up beside Valerie.

"Well, that escalated," Valerie said with a chuckle. "Back to our old ways so soon."

"Hey, at least it was your fault, not mine." Robin winked, hands raised in fists.

*PHWOOT!* A round from a firearm slammed into the tree right next to Qwaza's head and an instant later Qwaza and the other aliens went to their knees, heads down in supplication.

"What's gotten you so riled up?" a male asked, stepping into the clearing. He was short with grey skin, and held a pistol at the ready. His body armor shot out in sharp angles, each point glimmering in the hazy light. His skin wasn't actually grey, Valerie realized, but covered in tattoos.

"Master Platu, we have a visitor," Qwaza said, motioning to Valerie with his head still bowed. "She says she's here for the Damu Michezo."

"Is that so?" Platu stepped forward, analyzing the grey blood streaked across Qwaza's cheek and the crack in his carapace. "Looks like she dealt you some damage. Might be worth betting on, then."

Qwaza grumbled but nodded, bringing his head up to stare at her in confusion. He must've noticed the way her cheek had healed from his cut. "She can certainly hold her own."

Platu beamed at Valerie. "Not everyone can enter the Damu Michezo, only those with an invitation. That said, you seem resourceful. What if I told you I know someone who can help? I've never seen your kind, but if you're here to fight, I'm sure you'll blend in."

"What do you mean?" Valerie asked, finally lowering her guard.

"The Damu Michezo is a contest among alien races," he explained. "Of course, the winner is almost always from the same planet, which only fuels the passion with which other planets send their fighters. It's a bloodbath, one I'd advise you to stay clear of."

"I can't do that," she replied.

He nodded. "I thought as much, which is why I'm going to arrange to place a bet on you. Not to win, but to make it at least a few levels toward the top."

"Thank you?"

"No, thank *you*. If you fight down there half as well as you did just now, you'll double my earnings for the month."

"Qwaza mentioned a shuttle?" Robin interjected.

"Ah, right." Platu signaled to Qwaza. "Up with you. Who flew out today?"

"Some of the tourists, a male from the—"

"No, fool. The pilot. My Skulla pilot. Which one?"

"My apologies." He glanced at one of his companions, and only by the tone of her voice did Valerie realize it was a female when she spoke.

"The one you told to never set foot here again," the female said to Platu. "I think his name was Deleck. Said something about him sleeping with—"

"That'll do," he interrupted, turning a slighter darker shade under the tattoos. "There you have it. You find this Deleck on his shuttle and you've found your way to the infamous Damu Michezo, and likely your death."

"How exactly are we supposed to find the shuttle?" Robin asked, glancing at the sky. "There's a lot of area up there in which to look for a shuttle, and I don't think we have time to dawdle."

"Quite right, quite right. You'll have to fly fast if you want to catch them. They left not so long ago." Platu smiled and took his rifle, starting to draw in the red dirt that had settled around the cracked tree. "This is us," he drew a circle, "and this was their trajectory." Now pointing at the system's star, he told them, "Head in that direction at a slight angle to the left and you'll be on track, more or less."

"More or less," Valerie repeated, her stomach already knotting. She hated the idea of not reaching the contest in time, therefore failing in her first mission. She had never failed before, however, so she took a deep breath and pulled her thoughts together, blocking out the bad.

She thanked them and returned with Robin to the ship, ready to do her best to find a random shuttle somewhere out there.

Robin gave her a look that expressed the same doubt she herself was having, but said only, "Sounds like this'll be fun. Like a treasure lost at sea, only in this case it's space."

"And the treasure is a random name given to us by what appears to be a slaver."

Robin nodded. "Exactly. The uncertainty is what makes it fun, right? I mean, worst-case scenario, Colonel Walton kicks us out of Bad Company and then we fly off to some other planet and become assassins for hire. Doesn't sound so horrible, does it?"

"Don't joke about that," Valerie pleaded, laughing. "You're going to tell me you left your parents on Earth to come up here and defend the universe, but would settle for becoming some mercenary?"

"I said 'assassin,' which sounds way cooler," Robin replied, then frowned. "And no. Shut up."

"Then let's be sure we succeed." Valerie clasped her friend's shoulder and they entered the ship, ready to get down to business.

## 2

**Space: The *Singlaxian Grandeur***

"We have a visual," Bob said, leaning back in his chair and gesturing at the screen before him. There was the blip of a ship out there, still in the distance, but likely the one they were after—their key to finding and entering the Damu Michezo.

"Earth's first step toward competing in an intergalactic fight club," Robin said with a chuckle. "Well, that we know of, anyway."

"That little contest back on the ship with Colonel Walton was a bit of a fight club," Corporal Flynn pointed out. "But it wasn't intergalactic, was it?"

Valerie frowned and everyone looked at her hesitantly, which made her even more annoyed. She didn't like to think about that, and especially didn't like to remember how it had felt to have her kneecap broken. She had healed from all manner of gunshots and stabs back on Earth, but a broken kneecap was its own level of misery.

She'd have to remember to not square off against Colonel Walton anytime soon, or if she did, to strike first and show no mercy. Seeing as he was pretty much her supervisor now, in a sense, she doubted that would be happening anytime soon.

"What's the plan, boss?" Sergeant Garcia asked, breaking the tension.

Valerie stared out at the system, amazed by the vastness of their undertaking. She hadn't spent much time in space, her only experience thus far being when she had traveled with Colonel Terry Henry Walton to reunite with Michael and finally meet the glorious Bethany Anne.

Somehow she had imagined that a new galaxy would be different. Instead of vast stretches of darkness and more stars, she had half-expected to be able to see every planet in a display of multicolored orbs for her viewing pleasure.

What she got instead was the view past the transporter ship of a planet that from this distance didn't look so different from Earth. The system's star shone brightly beyond it, casting most of this side of the planet in darkness.

"Is that what a transport ship looks like?" she asked.

"That's her, all right." Bob pressed the screen and made a few swiping motions. "We don't know much about the people this far out, but here's what the Etheric Federation has. Hell, we've never had a team out here. I don't even know where to begin."

"Best way to learn the lay of the land is by befriending a local," Valerie replied.

"And if the locals are giant lizard men?" Garcia asked. "I'm not exactly ready for that sort of friend."

Valerie turned to Robin, who was at her side, and said, "I think we can handle it."

"Lizard men?" Robin scoffed. "Just be happy they aren't lizard women. More aggressive, I hear."

"Are you making that up? There are no actual lizard people in space, are there?"

She laughed. "No, Bob, I don't think so, though I actually have no idea." She nodded, then added, "Follow her, for now. No reason to scare them off just yet."

"Yeah, got it," Bob replied, then leaned forward, and coughed. "Uh, shit. Is that… Yup. That's another ship attached to the far side."

"And another one coming," Garcia pointed to another object moving in from the opposite side of the transporter ship, making it difficult to see. "A friendly chat, you think?"

"Dammit, looks like we're going to have to find out." Valerie took a seat next to Bob and said, "I'll take the controls."

Bob glared, but held up his hands. *Typical Bob*, Valerie thought as she started maneuvering the *Grandeur* around the transport to get a better look at the approaching shuttle.

"Anyone here know a damn thing about spaceships?" she asked.

Everyone mumbled, but Garcia spoke up. "Not a thing, but if I had to bet I'd wager that's an attack vessel."

"And I'd wager you're right," she replied. "I'd also point out that we don't like attack vessels moving in on transport ships that are supposed to be the key to our mission. That being the case…"

With a surge of energy at the thrill of the fight running

through her veins, she increased her speed and readied her weapons.

## Civilian Transport Shuttle

Kalan knew he was in trouble the moment the airlock opened and the six Pallicons marched aboard, weapons drawn.

Up until then, it had been a fairly uneventful flight. He'd barely made it to the transport in time for departure to Tol, and when he'd seen how crowded the shuttle was, he'd almost wished he hadn't. He'd even strongly considered getting off and transferring his ticket to the next shuttle, but that would have meant missing his appointment, which would mean he wouldn't get the job. And he badly needed the job.

So instead of getting off, he'd squeezed himself into a seat and waited for the transport to lift.

The passengers were mostly Skulla, but there were a few Pallicons too. He'd always envied Pallicons a little. They were shapeshifters, and Kalan would have given anything to be able to do that.

It would be nice to be something other than a muscle-bound six-and-a-half-foot-tall gray-skinned freak every once in a while. To not have everyone cast a cautious eye at him anytime he walked into a room.

Kalan hadn't been to the planet Tol before, but he'd spent most of his life in the Vurugu system. Six planets revolved around an ancient star. The outer five had been terraformed and were populated mostly by Skulla, a species that decorated their skins—faces included—with countless tattoos as part of their strange religion.

Skulla only stood about four feet tall and were thin creatures, but they made up for their small size with razor-sharp wits, and were often ruthless.

The planet closest to the center of the cluster was the home of the Pallicons. It was almost impossible to spot them when they were shapeshifting, but Kalan'd had a lot of practice. The key was to stare at the edges. Focus on a single hair or a knuckle; something small and specific. If you watched a shapeshifted Pallicon for ten or twenty seconds like that you'd see a tiny flicker, and then you'd know.

He was starting to relax about an hour into the flight when the ship was attacked. Less than five minutes later, the six Pallicons boarded, through the airlock, their weapons drawn.

"This ship is hereby commandeered in the name of the Bandian!" one of them shouted.

A murmur ran through the passengers when they heard that name, and Kalan raised an eyebrow. If these guys really were from the Bandian, that was bad news indeed.

While the first Pallicon spoke the others spread out, one heading toward the cockpit while the rest dispersed to either end of the transport to cover the passengers.

Kalan watched all this silently. He carefully controlled his breathing, and reminded himself not to get involved unless he absolutely had to. This wasn't prison. He didn't need to step up to every tough guy who crossed his path. He didn't have to prove himself.

Yet, as he watched the four of them work, Kalan grew

more uncomfortable. He spotted their weapons, handheld Tralen-14s. Those were not cheap, and they were difficult to get in this ass-end of the galaxy. These guys were well funded.

The other thing that worried him was that they seemed absolutely disinterested in the jewelry most of the Skulla wore. If they weren't there to rob the passengers, probably they were there to steal the ship itself—which wouldn't be good news for the passengers.

Maybe the hijackers would keep them alive and try to ransom them back to their families, but it seemed more likely the Pallicons would escort them out the nearest airlock at the earliest opportunity.

The small Skulla female next to him clasped her hands on her lap, and it was clear she was trying to keep them from shaking. She kept shifting her gaze between the six Pallicons, eyes darting back and forth frantically.

Kalan leaned over to her. "It's going to be okay."

As soon as he'd said the words he regretted them. He didn't make a promise unless he intended to keep it, and now that he'd told the female things were going to work out, he was going to have to do whatever it took to make sure he wasn't a liar.

The female kept her eyes on the hijackers. "I don't know. The Bandian doesn't leave witnesses."

Kalan had no idea what the average Skulla lifespan was, but this female had to be near the end of it. Her facial tattoos were so faded it was difficult to imagine what they'd once been.

"Hey, you ever seen one of my kind?" he asked.

The female reluctantly turned toward him, which had

been his goal. If she stopped looking at the hijackers, maybe she'd stop thinking about them for moment or two.

"No, I don't think I have."

He smiled. "I'm not surprised. There aren't a lot of us, especially not in this part of the system. As far as I know, there are only two of us *Gah'har'zakanew* in the system."

Her eyes narrowed as she tried to repeat the name back to him. "*Gah'har*-what?"

"You can call us the 'Grayhewn.' Everyone else does." He nodded toward the Pallicon at the far end of the ship. "Point is, they've probably never heard of my kind either, which means they don't know what kind of trouble they're in right now."

He winked.

Kalan hoped he sounded more confident than he felt. He was used to fighting against long odds, but Pallicons were scrappy even when they *weren't* carrying cutting-edge weaponry.

The hijackers had gathered the flight crew outside the cockpit and had them on their knees, weapons to their heads. If Kalan was going to act, it had to be now.

"Wish me luck," he said to the old female. Then he drew a deep breath, unstrapped his safety harness, and started to rise.

A loud chirping sound came through the open cockpit door, and Kalan had piloted enough ships to recognize it. That was the proximity alert.

The Pallicon who had been shouting orders smiled.

"That's their friends, isn't it?" the old Skulla next to Kalan asked.

Kalan didn't have time to wonder *how* the old female

recognized the sound of a proximity alert from forty feet away. Instead, he focused on the fact that she was right. Likely it was a large ship that would take the small transport shuttle aboard, effectively making it impossible to locate once they'd stripped it.

If the larger ship had arrived, they were lost. The thing that got Kalan out of his seat was the thought of these Pallicons' bosses boarding the transport to find the hijackers beaten silly and Kalan's smiling face looking down on them.

As he was getting out of his seat, the Pallicon in the cockpit called to the others, "Uh, we've got a problem. There's not one ship outside, there's two. And the other one seems to be attacking ours."

### The *Singlaxian Grandeur*

"You're not going to open fire, are you?" Bob asked, aghast.

"Just a precaution," she replied, pressing more buttons. With a sigh of exasperation she added, "How do we hail them?"

"Hail?" Garcia asked.

"You know, send them a message."

Bob leaned forward and hit the large button that—now that Valerie looked at it—was clearly a talk symbol, then the image of the ship on the screen. "That'll send a message in their direction."

"And the implant chips will translate?"

He nodded. "Like on the planet we just left. Unless it's a

very obscure language, the chip will translate automatically."

She nodded. The message button had now lit up, so she assumed it was live.

"This is Valerie of the *Singlaxian Grandeur*—"

"The grandest little ship you ever did see," mumbled Bob in a sing-song way.

She glared at him, then continued, "We are new here, but have reasons to see this transport vessel on its way. If you are hostile, we must warn you… We can be hostile back."

They waited for a moment, Valerie's fingers massaging the triggers, and then the response came. Not as a message, however, but as a barrage of blasts from three mounted railguns, one on each wing and one at the bow.

"At least it's an answer we can understand," Garcia quipped as Valerie threw the ship into an evasive maneuver, spinning around the shots and then counterattacking with her own weapons.

As a blast hit and the blue energy field that protected the *Grandeur* glimmered, she was clearly reminded that out here she could die like the rest of them. If the *Grandeur* exploded, she was damn sure her body wouldn't heal itself from the effects of space. Or if it somehow could, she imagined a lifetime of torture as she suffocated and burned —or whatever happened in space to one's body—and then regenerated, only to repeat the process all over.

Now *that* would be hell.

She had to ensure it didn't come to that. Luckily for her she had flown plenty of antigravity Pods back on Earth, and this wasn't so different. Faster and equipped with more firepower, but other than that... She was getting the hang of it.

By the time the enemy ship had recalibrated and was ready for the next wave of shots she had already dived, avoiding the attack and coming around to blast the enemy in the underbelly.

Their shields held momentarily, and then they were gone like a fizzle of a candle being snuffed. The enemy ship maneuvered out of the way of her next shot but she pursued, knowing that it was only a matter of time.

## 3

---

**Civilian Transport Shuttle**

Kalan didn't consider himself much of a strategist when it came to fighting, but he did know this much: if your enemy's looking the other way, it's a good time to hit him.

As the Pallicons reacted to the mysterious appearance of another ship, Kalan turned to the old female next to him and nodded toward the oversized bag at her feet. "You wouldn't happen to have a handgun in there, would you?"

"Sorry, I left it in my nightstand."

The response was so deadpan that Kalan didn't know if she was joking.

"Okay, guess I'll do this the other way then." He winked once more, then stalked down the aisle.

The guy closest to Kalan, the one whose job was almost certainly to watch the passengers on this end of the shuttle, was so distracted by the news from the cockpit that he didn't notice Kalan coming. Kalan shook his head at the gross dereliction of duty as he approached. You had to be *really* bad at your job to miss a six-foot-five gray-skinned brute coming at you. Maybe the kid would learn a valuable lesson from this—assuming he survived.

Kalan knew he would have to move quickly once the fighting started. There were fifty-odd passengers aboard this shuttle, all cramped into a space designed to allow for maximum profit. If even one of those six well-armed Pallicons got spooked and started shooting wildly, things would go badly for the passengers very fast.

He eyed the hatch that led to the cargo hold. If he could get down there, any shots they fired at him would be aimed *away* from the passengers. That became his goal, but first he had to deal with this distracted hijacker.

Kalan waited until he'd almost reached him, then gently cleared his throat.

The hijacker turned in time to see Kalan's massive fist rushing toward his face. When it connected, he collapsed in a heap.

Pallicons were easy enough to take down if you caught them unaware—and if you could punch with the force of a small handgun—but Kalan knew he wouldn't have that luxury with the other five. When their friend hit the ground, the four in the aisle were already turning toward him.

He reached down and grabbed the fallen man's weapon, then sprinted toward the hatch to the cargo hold, arms pumping as he dashed past the rows of passengers. They stared at him with their tattooed faces, clearly unsure whether he was their savior or another threat.

Kalan wasn't so sure himself. If the hijackers got their Tralen-14s up and started shooting before he reached the cargo area, every passenger on the transport better hope the Pallicons' marksmanship was better than their ability to secure a hostage situation. A single stray shot could blow a hole in any of the passengers.

When he reached the cargo hatch, he glanced back. The old Skulla female who'd been sitting next to him was watching wide-eyed, so he gave her one last wink before ducking through the doorframe and down the ladder to the hold below.

There wasn't a lot of room to maneuver down there, which Kalan took as a positive. Close quarters meant they wouldn't be able to surround him.

He wove through the crates and cases, and found an advantageous spot between two larger ones. It allowed him a bit of darkness to hide in, but it also didn't pin him down too much.

The first head peeked into Kalan's line of sight and Kalan immediately fired, dropping the Pallicon. Two down, four to go.

No second head appeared. Instead, Kalan heard the click of feet on the metal floor scurrying past his location.

This one was using his shape-changing ability, which was going to make things a bit more difficult.

Kalan thought, *These Pallicon sonsabitches could be tricky.*

He waited until he was sure the male had passed his hiding place, then he drew a deep breath and stepped into the aisle. He kept his handgun trained on the deck.

Sure enough, the Pallicon was waiting. He'd changed his shape to make four short legs grow underneath him so he could lay on his back as he walked.

He spotted Kalan a split second after Kalan spotted

him. Thankfully for Kalan he was faster than the Pallicon, and he blasted a hole in his chest.

Kalan shook his head, almost feeling sorry for the poor bastard. When he'd reshaped himself into a monstrosity with four legs coming out of his back, he'd probably never figured he'd stay like that for eternity.

The communicator on the Pallicon's belt flashed, and a voice came through. "Everything all right down there, Uunard?"

Kalan paused for a moment, then reminded himself he was probably going to die on this shuttle anyway. Might as well have a little fun first.

He grabbed the communicator and held it to his mouth. "Everything's good. We could use a little help, though. We took him down, but he got me in the leg. Hurts like a son of a bitch. This gray guy's as big as a yanecat."

The reply was instantaneous, and it didn't sound happy. "Suck it up, shape yourself a new leg, and get over here. We've got fifty passengers to corral and there's a damn battle going on outside, so we don't have time for you to cry into your soup."

Kalan paused for another moment, then decided to give it one more try. "Okay, I get it. Could you at least toss me down a medkit? I'm bleeding all over the place."

The reply sounded both disgusted and resigned. "Hang on."

Thirty seconds later a male carrying a medkit appeared in the hatch. Kalan promptly shot him in the head, then in the torso for good measure.

The communicator chirped again. "Uh, Uunard, what's going on down there?"

Kalan struggled to keep the smile out of his voice as he answered, "The big guy wasn't dead after all. I think we're going to need another medkit."

There was a long pause before the voice came through the comm again. "Listen, you stupid piece of shift-waste, in about three minutes this transport is going to be swarming with three dozen Pallicons. If you give yourself up, I'll end you quick. Otherwise you're going to be a long time dying. Do you know what we do to beings who kill Pallicons?"

"Do you bring them medkits?"

Kalan didn't wait around to hear the hijacker's response. Instead, he crept up the ladder and carefully stuck his head through the hatch.

As he'd suspected, the two remaining Pallicons were nowhere in sight. Most likely they'd retreated to the cockpit. The passengers still sat stone-faced and afraid, as if the hijackers were holding guns to each of their heads.

Kalan didn't blame them. They weren't accustomed to this sort of threat to their lives. Sadly, the same couldn't be said for Kalan.

He stalked down the aisle toward the cockpit, knowing that no matter the outcome of this fight, he and the rest of the passengers were likely to die soon. As long as he took a few of these shapeshifting assholes with him, he'd die content.

When he reached the cockpit, someone stepped out and glared at him. Kalan almost laughed as he saw his own face staring back at him. The Pallicon had shifted into a perfect copy of him.

"If you're trying to intimidate me, you should have shifted into someone less handsome," he pointed out. It was an old Pallicon trick, Kalan knew. An average guy hesitated to punch himself in the face, even if he wasn't the one wearing it.

Unfortunately for the Pallicons, Kalan wasn't the average guy.

"I've always wondered if I could beat myself in a fight," he said with a smile. "This is going to be fun."

### The *Singlaxian Grandeur*

Each time Valerie missed the ship, she became increasingly worried this whole space-shooting thing wasn't for her. Give her a gun and a sword and she could take on an army by herself, but flying around space with only this hunk of metal to protect her while shooting crazy technology-driven laser beams at another ship? The idea was almost ludicrous.

And yet, it was exactly what was required of her if she were to pull this off.

"Oh, I have an idea!" Bob said, clinging onto the armrests of his chair as the ship spun again. "Try hitting them with the next one."

"Try biting your own ear," she replied. "But until you're able, shut your stupid fucking mouth."

"Anyone else feel like we're in a hostile work environment?"

"SHUT UP!" Robin and Garcia said as one, and this time he listened.

Valerie was about to thank them, but instead she let out a yelp of excitement. A hit had finally landed on an enemy ship, tearing one of the wings. The ship was veering back and forth, overcompensating and then turning back toward them, and she fired again. With a series of connecting shots, the enemy ship was blasted into debris.

"Let's hope those were the bad guys," Garcia said with a chuckle. "I'd hate to find out we just blew up the local leadership's personal guard or something worse."

"They shot at us, ignoring my hail," Valerie countered. "Of course they were the bad guys."

He shrugged. "Either way, they're dead now."

"They were the bad guys," she mumbled, swerving to avoid the debris of the enemy ship and then turning back toward the transport.

When she pulled up to the small ship she tried hailing it, but no response came—not even in the form of gunfire.

"Don't blow it away," Bob suggested.

"Oh, you were able to successfully bite your ear?" she asked. "Let's see it, then."

He glared, actually tried, and then glared again when he realized how stupid that had looked.

"Yeah, I didn't think so." She raised her eyebrows. "Which makes me wonder… Why are you talking?"

Robin cleared her throat. "I'm not sure if this is like two cats playing or two people flirting—it's honestly confusing —so would you two stop and focus on the situation at hand?"

"Sorry." Valerie blushed and maneuvered in closer, noticing a docking bay near on the transport ship. "Looks like we're boarding her. We need to be sure she hasn't been taken over by the enemy, because we need to get to that competition and right now this is our best bet."

Docking wasn't as easy as she had hoped, but they made

a direct connection so there was no need for suits or pressurization chambers. They went in with everyone on guard, weapons at the ready.

Even without such things as movies back on Earth— those had only been introduced to Valerie in space, since Earth had lost much technology since the Great Collapse— Valerie was able to imagine all sorts of monstrous aliens within. Her mind went to strange places, like a being made of leaves, or maybe there would be a whole cadre of giant spiders. That really made her wonder what they'd be up against, but also made her laugh.

"Something's funny?" Robin whispered at her side, preparing to turn the corner into the main cabin of the ship.

"Just... Odd that *we* were the monsters back home. I mean vampires and Weres... We were essentially boogeymen, only real. Now look at us, walking into a ship that could be filled with slime monsters or massive eyeballs that walk, for all we know."

Robin frowned, then shook her head. "No, not funny. Ironic, yet terrifying."

"But you're ready, right? I can count on you?"

With a nod and a smile, Robin gestured. "After you."

Valerie smiled and darted out of the hallway, only to freeze where she stood, mouth open as she stared in confusion.

What she found was no monster in the sense that she had imagined. Instead, the room was full of short tattooed people like the one she had seen on the planet, and two tall gray-skinned men fighting each other. What was odd, though, was that as far as she could tell there was no difference between the two. It was almost like watching a man fight himself in the mirror.

Not knowing how to proceed, she held up a hand for the others to halt. They would see how this played out, and only then interfere.

## 4

**Civilian Transport Shuttle**

Kalan threw another punch and was relieved to see the Pallicon wearing his face go down. That alien could take a hit. He'd withstood three of Kalan's best shots before finally falling to the deck.

He was vaguely aware that the airlock had opened during the fight, but he'd been too busy taking the shapeshifter down to pay it much attention. Now he saw four creatures watching him.

One look told him they weren't Pallicons, or at least not Pallicons in their natural form.

He smiled sheepishly as the four gun-toting intruders marched down the aisle toward him. They weren't the biggest beings he'd ever seen, but based on the way they carried themselves and the weapons they held, these four meant business. He picked a spot on the dark-haired woman's head and stared at it while she approached, watching for the telltale signs. By the time she reached him, he was confident she wasn't a shapeshifter.

"Drop the handgun," the woman ordered.

Kalan quickly complied, letting the Tralen-14 slip from his hand with a pang of regret. He had really liked that weapon.

The woman looked at the body at Kalan's feet, then up at him. Then back at the body. "What the hell is this? Is he your twin brother or something?"

"No, ma'am," he said, his hands still high in the air. "He's a Pallicon. They're shapeshifters."

In truth, the term "shapeshifters" didn't accurately describe the beings. Young ones, like the six who'd attempted to hijack the shuttle, were limited to changing their shapes. However, as Pallicons grew older, they became more resilient. Kalan had seen a middle-aged Pallicon shrug off a gunshot wound like it was nothing. The creature had simply reshaped himself so the wound no longer existed.

Some said that elderly Pallicons were nearly unkillable; that you couldn't give them an injury they couldn't shift away. But the culture was so secretive it was impossible to distinguish truth from legend.

The brown-haired woman cast her gaze around the ship, then settled it back on Kalan. "You'd better start explaining. What happened here?"

Kalan opened his mouth to answer, but before he could he heard a voice behind him.

"I'll tell you what happened. This one saved our lives!" The old Skulla female marched down the aisle toward them. "He unbuckled his harness, got out of his seat, and kicked their asses."

The woman raised an eyebrow. "Sounds like our kind of guy. I'm Valerie." She gestured toward her three companions. "The good-looking one is Robin. The other two are Garcia and Flynn."

Kalan nodded a greeting. "I'm Kalan of Clan Gah'har'zakanew." When he saw the looks on their faces, he quickly added, "Kalan Grayhewn is fine."

"Kalan's a hero," the old female said. "He took down six Pallicons all by himself."

Kalan tilted his head, remembering something. "Actually I only took down five. I got so caught up fighting my handsome lookalike that I forgot about the leader."

Suddenly the sixth Pallicon rushed out of the cockpit, handgun raised and a snarl on his face.

Valerie moved so fast Kalan could barely track her movement. She whirled toward the male in a blur and lashed out, her hand striking him in the face so hard he slammed into the bulkhead and slid unconscious to the deck.

"Holy shit," Kalan muttered. He'd seen some things in his time, but he'd *never* seen anyone move like that.

"Why'd you go so easy on him?" Robin asked.

Valerie shrugged. "I figured we might want to question him."

Kalan took a small step backward. If that was going *easy*, he didn't want to see this woman go all-out.

Ten minutes later he was on the *Singlaxian Grandeur*. They'd invited him aboard in a tone that made it clear it was mere politeness that kept it from being an order. After what he'd seen Valerie do, he wasn't about to argue. His only regret was that he hadn't had time to thank the old Skulla female for sticking up for him.

Garcia took him to a small cabin furnished with only a table and a few chairs, and told him to wait for Valerie. He did just that for the next twenty minutes. The wait didn't bother him. He'd had a lot of practice over the years, and he'd come to enjoy the company of his own thoughts.

He spent the time thinking about what he might do next once this weird interview was over. He'd have to scrounge for new job prospects now that he'd missed his other interview. Starting over didn't sound appealing. There were plenty of friends who could get him work if he was willing to step outside the law…

But no. He'd promised himself he wouldn't go that route, and he intended to keep that promise.

He was so lost in his own thoughts that he started when the door slid open and Valerie and Garcia sauntered in. Valerie took the seat across from him and looked him in the eye, while Garcia remained standing and hovered behind her.

"Kalan Grayhewn," Valerie said. "Let's talk."

"Ready when you are." He didn't mean the comment to come off as snarky, but this was beginning to feel like an interrogation.

"First question. Where'd you learn to fight like that? You a military man?"

"No, ma'am. Maybe in another life I would have gone that way, but in this one I'm a saby."

Valerie's eyes narrowed. "I thought you said you were a Grayhewn. Which is it?"

Kalan leaned forward in his seat, trying to figure out if the woman was joking. When he realized she wasn't, he began to wonder where the hell she was from that she hadn't heard of sabies.

"It's short for 'SEDE baby', ma'am." He waited for the light of recognition to come into her eyes. When it didn't, he figured he'd better explain further. "The Swarthian Extended Detention Environment. 'SEDE.' It's a prison. Largest in the galaxy, or at least that's their claim. My mother was incarcerated there when I was born."

"Ah, 'SEDE baby.' I get it."

"Thing is, SEDE has a policy that any kids born in their prison have to stay there until they're eighteen. In theory it's to deter people from having kids aboard SEDE. Hope is, no parent wants to put a kid through that kind of hell. In reality, we end up with a bunch of kids who age out of the system with no skills other than the ones they learned in the galaxy's toughest prison."

"And you're one of those?" Valerie asked.

Kalan nodded. "I know half the scumbags in the system. Shit, I grew up with most of them. But I'd like to think I picked up a few other skills, too, the kind that would make me employable. I'm a pretty decent pilot. I fix engines. I'm definitely not afraid to get my hands dirty. Seems potential employers don't share my optimistic viewpoint, though. They tend to shy away from anyone with the word SEDE on their record, earned or not. I've been out five years, and I've yet to find consistent work."

He tried to read her eyes as she listened to him, but he found he couldn't. There was something odd about her, something that felt different than any being he'd ever encountered.

"Wait," she interjected. "You said 'aboard' SEDE."

"Yes, ma'am. SEDE's a prison ship. Stays on the move, and its flight plan is top secret. Makes breaking out nigh impossible."

"Geez, a flying prison," Garcia observed, shaking his head in amazement.

Valerie said, "You've got a choice to make. You say you're a pilot. I'll bet the company who runs those shuttles would jump at the chance to hire a hero who just saved one of their ships from shapeshifting hijackers. Play your cards right, and I'll bet you could build a nice little career for yourself."

He sat up a bit straighter. He hadn't considered that. Being a shuttle pilot would be boring as dust, but it would be a steady job. "You said I had a choice. What's the other option?"

"My team and I aren't from around here."

"You're kidding," he said dryly.

"We have a job to do in this system, and doing it will require us to get up close and personal with the locals. We could use a guy who knows the lay of the land. Someone who can stop me before I offend a whole culture by waving hello with the wrong hand or something."

He considered that a moment. "I'm flattered, ma'am, but I'm not from around here either. I've spent most of my free life on the other side of the system."

Valerie shrugged. "You said you know half the scum in the system. And it doesn't hurt that you can handle yourself in a fight."

"Huh." He thought a moment. "And who exactly would I be working for? You'd be giving me my orders, but who gives you yours?"

She leaned forward and smiled. "The good guys."

For some strange reason, he believed her. "That's how it is? I don't get to know who I'm working for?"

"You're working for me. That should be enough. I'll give you more details if and when they become relevant to the job." She paused. "The only thing I'll add is this... My intel says there's a bully in this planetary system. We're going to smack him down. You want to help?"

Kalan sighed. "I've always hated bullies."

"Is that a yes?"

He paused a moment, then smiled. "I guess the shuttle companies will still be hiring when this is over."

She held out a hand. "Welcome aboard, Grayhewn."

He took her hand and she shook it in a strange up and down motion, not the backward-and-forward method he was used to. She really *wasn't* from around here.

"So how the hell does a prisoner learn to be a pilot?" she asked.

Kalan chuckled. "That's a strange story. It was all because a Yollin prisoner missed dinner. You see—"

Valerie's communicator beeped, interrupting him.

Bob's voice came through. "Valerie, we have a problem."

## 5

The *Singlaxian Grandeur*

Kalan, Valerie, and Garcia made their way to the flight deck, where they found Bob frowning at the controls. He looked up when he heard them enter, and his beady eyes focused on Valerie.

He started explaining the situation without preamble. "Turns out those shapeshifting freaks really put the fear of God into the guys flying the transport. The pilot's refusing to continue to the planet. He's sitting in his seat waiting. Keeps saying 'he'll be back for us,' whoever 'he' is."

"Huh." Kalan gestured toward the transport on the display. "One of the hijackers said something about 'the Bandian' when they took the ship. I thought he was just trying to scare us, but maybe he really is their boss."

"You've heard of him?" Valerie asked.

Kalan nodded. "He's a warlord from Tol, or at least he used to be. Now he controls half the damn system. And his rise to power wasn't exactly peaceful, if you know what I mean."

Valerie sighed. "Regardless, we still need somebody to fly that transport to the Damu Michezo. You up for it, Grayhewn?"

Kalan grimaced. He'd forgotten about the tournament. The planet would be a madhouse, even if they did manage to get there in one piece. "You guys aren't mixed up with the Damu Michezo, are you?"

Valerie grinned. "Trying to be."

A whistle escaped Kalan's lips. "I've seen more prison fights than I can remember, and I've been in more than I'd like. No way I'd set foot in the Damu Michezo, though. That's some crazy shit. If you're smart, you'll stay far away."

"Thanks for the advice." The smile slipped from Valerie's face. "You gonna fly the transport or not?"

A few minutes later Kalan found himself in the cockpit of the transport ship, trying to make sense of the controls. He'd flown a few ships in his time, but the layout of this one was a bit odd.

The pilot of the transport glared at him from the seat Valerie had cuffed him to. "Don't be an idiot. The Bandian doesn't let prisoners escape. If we run, it'll only make it worse. He'll find us and kill us."

Kalan raised an eyebrow. "You'd prefer to have him kill us here? Make it easy for him?"

The captain lowered his voice to a near-whisper. "These dumbass passengers? Yeah, sure, they're dead either way. But you and I are pilots. The Bandian needs pilots."

Kalan resisted the urge to smack the living hell out of this guy. He'd never work for the Bandian. He'd done a lot of things he wasn't proud of in his life, but that was a line he wouldn't cross. "You know what I've never understood? The guy's called 'Warlord Nobir.' Why's he need a nickname like 'the Bandian?'"

The pilot scoffed. "A nickname, a title—call it what you will. Don't tell me you never heard the legend of the Bandians."

Kalan shrugged. "I grew up sheltered."

"It's the name of an ancient race of warriors from this part of the system, long extinct. Warlord Nobir uses their name to remind us of the glory possible for a race even from a backwater place like this."

"Huh. Sounds like you're a big fan of this Bandian guy."

"It's better than the alternative. Join the Etheric Federation? No, thank you!"

Kalan didn't respond, since he didn't have much of an opinion on politics. All he knew was that he hated the Bandian.

"Excuse me? I just wanted to thank you again."

The voice came from behind him, and Kalan turned to see the elderly Skulla female who'd sat next to him. The thankful look on her face made him smile.

"My name's Esur, by the way," she added.

"I'm Kalan." He paused, a little embarrassed. "There's no need for thanks, ma'am. I was trying to buy us a little time. It was Valerie and her crew who saved us."

"We wouldn't have lived long enough for them to save us if you hadn't acted." She shook her head, and a hint of sadness entered her voice. "When I think of what almost happened…. And on the way to the Damu Michezo, too!"

Kalan tilted his head in surprise. "You're a fan?"

"Of the Damu Michezo? Of course! I save up all year to come on this trip. Have you ever been?"

"No, ma'am. I've just heard the stories."

Her eyes glinted with delight. "Ah, it's so much better than you can imagine. There's nothing like the sound of a limb being torn from a competitor's body or the way the stadium hums with excitement when both fighters are near death. And the seats I got this year! I'll bet I'll get sprayed with blood before the end of the first match!"

Kalan forced himself to smile and nod politely. These Skulla were seriously weird creatures. He looked back at the controls, and everything clicked into place. That handle on the left was the throttle! Of course.

He grabbed the comm unit and pressed the button. "Bob, you there? Tell Valerie I've got this thing figured out. I'm ready to fly when you are."

Valerie's voice was barely audible in the background. "It's about damn time."

"Uh, she says that's great," Bob said. "We'll follow you to the planet."

Kalan signed off and put his hands on the controls. It was time to fly this ship to Tol.

### The *Singlaxian Grandeur*

Valerie couldn't believe the turn of events. Not long ago she had been on Earth kicking butt and taking names.

Now she was escorting an alien ship through space to protect it from other aliens, all so that she could find the planet where an alien death match would be held.

Her mind was running wild with the type of enemy she might face there. Since her possibilities were still based on what she had seen out here and legends she'd heard on Earth, she was imagining strange half-dragon aliens or maybe lava monsters. It couldn't be all Skulla or these other creatures who had tried to hijack them. No, she knew her luck wasn't that good.

Kalan flew with the other group, but the Skulla group had sent over two of their tattooed shorties to help guide them in case they got lost and also to help with communications between the two ships.

It was too bad, because Valerie had really wanted to ride with Kalan. He seemed like a fun guy—for a super-tall gray-skinned alien.

"We sure we can trust them?" Bob said under his breath, glancing at the Skulla at the rear of the command deck. "I mean, look at those tattoos. When you meet someone with tattoos like that on Earth, you know they're trouble."

"You think I'm trouble?" Garcia asked.

"What? You have tattoos?"

Valerie was curious too, and glanced at the tall sergeant.

He smiled wide. "They're not in places you'd want to see, but yeah, of course I do. Got them to commemorate my mom and pa when they passed. An angel and a devil."

"Wait, you got tattoos of your parents...somewhere we wouldn't want to see?" Valerie laughed. "You're an odd one, Garcia."

"Hey, I was in a dark place. I was thinking, 'Man, I gotta put the thought of them behind me.' So—"

"You went with your behind," she finished, the realization hitting her and making her laugh twice as hard. A glance from the Skulla reminded her this wasn't the best time for merriment.

"Which is which?" Bob asked.

"My dad was the devil," Garcia answered. "Fucker used to hit me like he thought I was a *piñata*, until one day my mom hit him back. He stared at her like he had no idea what was going on, then just walked out of there. Strangest thing I ever saw."

"Thought he was making you tough," Bob said with a nod. "Shit, yeah! If I had a boy I'd beat him too."

WHACK!

"Ouch!" Bob held the back of his head and glared up at Valerie. "What the hell was that for?"

"Being an insensitive idiot," she replied. "You ever have a son and hit him, I'll come for you."

Bob's face went white at that, and he returned his attention to the controls, watching the screen for action. He seemed to be mumbling something, but Valerie let it go.

"Sorry to hear that, Garcia," she said, turning back to the big man. "How'd they go? If you want to share, I mean."

Garcia glanced down at Bob with a frown, then shrugged. "All that BS aside, my pa ended up giving his life to save mine. I was stupid, thought I could swim better than I could. River took him, but not before he got me to safety. I'll never forget that moment, the love in his eyes that almost took away all those other times."

"And your mom?"

"Mom… She loved the old bastard. Broke her heart to be away from him. Still, she stuck it through, was happy to see me raised. They were a bit older when they had me, so when she passed, the best explanation we got was old age. You know your parents?"

Valerie smiled, trying to recall her birth parents, but shook her head. Many of her memories from before the day she had been turned were a blur, though that wasn't always the case with vampires. Robin remembered her folks as if she had never left them, and had even gone on a journey to find and rescue them. Now they lived in New York, along with Sandra, Diego, and a lot of Valerie's other friends. Damn, she missed them.

But her parents? The best she could figure was the moment had been traumatic, plus the way the Duke and his vampires had indoctrinated her—forcing her to train like a soldier until she was a killing machine—must've caused the fog in her brain.

"Sorry. If I'd known…" He put a hand on her shoulder.

"Come on." She brushed the hand away and gave him a shrug. "We all have our sob stories, huh?"

She spared a look at Robin, who was leaning against the wall and staring at the ceiling in thought. Valerie imagined the woman was thinking about her parents, wondering if she had made the right choice coming out here. It was tough, Valerie knew. She had left people behind too. Hell, Sandra and Diego had just had their baby! It hurt to know she wouldn't be there to see that kid grow up, but they had a duty to Earth and would see it through.

No matter how much alien butt they had to kick to get it done.

Speaking of which... She leaned forward, eyes on the display and the blinking red lights moving up behind them.

"They must've sent out a distress call," one of the Skulla said, stepping up next to her. She found it odd how his mouth moved differently from the words she heard, thanks to her translation chip.

"How many of them are out there?" Bob asked. "I mean, are we talking about some random bandits here, or...?"

"Or," the Skulla replied. "Meaning, we're all likely about to die." He shook his head, glaring at Valerie. "If you had just left us alone, this wouldn't be happening right now."

"Excuse me?" Robin stepped into his line of sight. "If not for us, you'd be their little bitches right now, as far as I understand it."

"Not the time, guys," Bob shouted, pointing at the display. He was right—those ships were closing faster than should have been possible.

"Okay, so they're well equipped," Valerie admitted. "Going up against...us. A team with very little flight experience, in a part of space no human has ever been."

"Hey, leader!" Garcia chimed in. "Aren't you supposed to be giving us a little pep talk or something?"

She considered this, then shook her head. "I think I'll focus on keeping us and our new friends alive instead."

With that she took the controls, focused on her time flying the Pods back home, and pulled around for the fight. She could hear cussing from the two Skulla, but the translator was having a hard time with it. That was fine, since she needed to concentrate on the task at hand.

Now that they were facing the oncoming trouble, they didn't need the display to show them the blips. They saw the ragged ships coming at them—at least a dozen. The transport ship was moving like a freight train through space, and was a sitting duck for their railguns.

"Hang on tight!" Valerie called and initiated her thrusters, diving to begin evasive maneuvers. Luckily she had a ship that was small enough to do so, with extra thrusters in place for this exact purpose.

"Turrets are ready," Bob said, glancing at her for the go-ahead.

"Get them locked and destroy these fucks," Garcia said, then let out an excited "Whoop!"

"Did he just whoop?" Bob asked with a roll of his eyes. "Who *does* that?"

"Me," Garcia said, slapping him upside the head in a playful yet loud way. "I also do *that* to jackasses. Want to keep being a jackass and see if I keep doing it?"

Bob grumbled, with a look to Valerie as if asking if she were going to intervene, but she only laughed.

"Hey," she said, "you want me to play mom, or you want me to save our asses and get us where we need to go? Gotta be one or the other."

They fired on the enemy ship before even spinning to get the lock on them, but Valerie was thinking hard about how they could end this fast.

"Any outside-the-box ideas?" she asked the team.

"Jump out there and tear their throats out," Robin offered. "I'll cut through their doors and rip 'em all to shreds." At a concerned glance from Valerie, she added, "Not the time for jokes. Noted."

Then it hit Valerie... *The other enemy ship, the one that had been docked to the transport shuttle.*

"Kalan, you there?" she said into the comm.

"We aren't going anywhere, not with those guys flying about. You got something for us?"

"I might. I want you to release that enemy ship. Send it into space, but only on my say-so. Do you have shields? The ship, I mean?"

He took a second, talking going on behind him, then he came back. "Enough for a couple hits, maybe. Why?"

"You're going to take a couple hits."

She turned to the transport, instead of focusing on the incoming fighters.

"Uh, aren't we supposed to be drawing fire away from them?" Flynn asked.

She smiled. "We'll have to hope this works."

An enemy fighter swept overhead and sprayed them with fire, but the shields shimmered as they absorbed the strikes.

"You *do* know we're not invincible either, right?" one of the Skulla asked, but she chuckled. Yes, she noticed the looks around her—as if she were insane. And no, she hadn't been in enough space battles to be an expert by any stretch of the imagination, but she had an idea.

"Turn off that ship's shields," she told Kalan, and he relayed the command. "On my mark, release it. Got it?"

"Any chance you're going to fill us in on what's happening soon?" Garcia asked. "I mean, I'm still into it and all, just…want to know."

"Better if I show you," she replied, and then swept around the transporter. "NOW!"

Sure enough, the abandoned enemy ship left the transporter with a kick and began to float, and the *Grandeur* positioned herself under it.

"We're taking hits!" Kalan called from the comm.

"Not for long," Valerie replied, glancing at her display to verify that the enemy were flying in a clustered formation. They were trained, but not for her.

She carefully came up to the floating ship, then put her thrusters into full acceleration. After moving back around to the other side of the transport she gave it another push and then, as they rounded the transport, she pulled back. *Grandeur* was still accelerating, but not as much. Meanwhile, the enemy ship went careening toward the formation.

She would've loved to know what the enemy was thinking as they saw their own ship coming at them. Maybe they were wondering if there were survivors, some of their own who had escaped but not managed to get the ship fully operational again.

Regardless, by the time they saw the *Grandeur* behind the other ship it was too late.

"Locked!" Bob announced.

"Fire," Valerie commanded.

With a series of blasts their warheads vanished into space, bursts of flame like retreating fireflies was all that was visible as they moved toward their targets. More blasts hit the transporter and a couple hit the *Grandeur*, but by then the warheads had made contact.

And like that, most of the enemy ships were debris. Forever to float through space, never to harm another Skulla or innocent transport ship.

"You saved us once, now do it again!" Kalan shouted

over the comm, but Valerie ignored him. She was doing her damned best.

Pulling behind the final attacking vessel, she sent one last barrage from the ship's blasters and shredded the enemy ship into scrap metal. Everyone on the *Grandeur* burst into cheers, and more sounded from the transport ship's connection.

She leaned over and announced into the comm, "Smooth ride from here, ladies and gentlemen. Sit back and enjoy it."

Bob was looking at her with wide eyes and nodding, impressed. Robin finally took her seat, where she leaned back and closed her eyes, while Garcia and the corporal were busy high fiving and fist-pounding each other. The Skulla were the only ones to approach Valerie.

"I'm sorry," the one from before said. He bowed his head. "I never should have doubted you. You were amazing."

"If you ever get bored and want to become a professional fighter pilot, our people could use someone like you," the second Skulla said. "Pays nicely, too."

She chuckled. "I already have a boss *and* a mission. Thank you, though."

"No, thank *you!*"

The Skulla returned to their seats at the rear of the command deck, and everyone watched as Valerie got the ship back on course. A large dark-green planet with some patches of water here and there became visible.

"Bob, can you take over?" Valerie asked.

He nodded and did so, and Valerie moved over to Robin. The younger woman peeked at her from behind a half-closed eyelid. Seeing that it was Valerie, she sat up, alert.

"We're really doing this, huh?" Valerie said.

Robin smiled. "Best time to change your mind is before you start beating the crap out of aliens. Of course, then you'd be a big wuss."

"You know me, I always back down." Valerie leaned against Robin's seat, arms folded across her chest as she watched the planet grow larger. "Nah, that's not what I meant. I just mean we've taken a side here. There's no going back, is there?"

"You and I aren't exactly diplomatic go-the-middle-route-and-be-sure-not-to-step-on-any-toes types," Robin replied. "Hell, if they wanted that they should've sent Sandra."

Valerie laughed, but shook her head. "You've seen Sandra the Caring Mom, but you didn't know her before. That girl kicked some serious ass in her day."

"Sure, if you say so. My point is, Michael knew you, and he knew what sending you out here would mean. I say we embrace it and be the best 'us' we can."

"You're wise beyond your years, you know that?"

"Shut up."

Valerie bit back a smile. "Hey, I mean it! It's simple logic. They were attacking a transport ship and were likely going to kill innocents, therefore they were bad. I get it. Still, it feels odd to show up and attack before we've gotten the lay of the land."

"Or lay of the planets, but I understand." Robin turned back to the screen to watch their approach.

"I just hope we're able to clearly differentiate enemy

from friend down there," Valerie stated, worry growing in the pit of her stomach. "Something tells me it won't be so simple."

"Given the nature of our work going forward," Robin stated with a nod of her head, "I'd count on it."

---

## 6

**Planet Tol: Civilian Transport Shuttle**

Kalan let go of the controls and exhaled in relief, a smile on his face. He turned to the pilot, still bound to the co-pilot's seat. "You gotta admit that was a pretty good landing, right?"

The pilot chuckled smugly. "Not bad, though you could have just let the autopilot land you."

The smile melted from Kalan's face. "Autopilot?" He'd searched the control panel top to bottom, but hadn't been able to figure out how to engage it. The pilot had told him there wasn't one. That had seemed far-fetched, but since he'd had no other choice he'd sweated through a manual landing after negotiating Tol's tumultuous upper atmosphere.

He glared at the pilot. "So let me get this straight. You let me think I had to manually land this thing, putting all our lives at risk just to fuck with me?"

The pilot shrugged. "Better to die in a transport crash than to have the Bandian catch up with us."

"The Bandian again, huh?" Kalan chuckled. "He may be vengeful, but even *he's* not going to take the time to personally attack our dumb transport. And if he does, we have Valerie watching our backs."

He had to admit he had been impressed with the way Valerie had defended the transport during the attack. Not many people would have risked their lives against such a formidable foe to protect strangers. Valerie had not only fought bravely, she'd fought well.

Kalan was beginning to suspect that he may have found that rarest of things: a leader worth following.

Not that he was the following type. He'd rather be left alone to do his own thing. But for the time being, he was glad he'd agreed to stay with Valerie and her crew. They seemed like a good bunch, although something about that Bob guy had been immediately irritating.

Now it was the pilot's turn to chuckle. "That attack? Those were just a few of the Bandian's lackeys. Had Warlord Nobir personally been here, it would have turned out differently."

Kalan wasn't convinced, but he was already sick of arguing with this idiot. He considered untying the pilot, but decided against it. Someone would be along eventually. Probably.

He exited the cockpit and nearly collided with Esur, who was hurrying for the exit hatch.

They chatted for a few minutes about the Damu Michezo, and then Esur excused herself. She didn't want to miss the first matches. Those were usually top contenders versus unworthy scrubs, so things tended to get especially bloody.

Kalan was surprised to find the beautiful Tralen-14 pistol still lying on the floor near the hatch where he'd dropped it on Valerie's orders. Seemed a shame to leave it there for the cleaning crew to find. Irresponsible, even. So he picked it up and put it on his belt.

After checking to ensure the passengers were okay, he headed onto the planet Tol for the first time.

His nose crinkled at the arid, hot breeze and the dust it carried. The landscape around him wasn't a desert, but he didn't see much in the way of plant life. He wondered if the dusty conditions were a result of over-farming or the side effect of a poorly-executed terraforming attempt. Either way, it didn't make for a pleasant environment. He hoped his stay on Tol would be short.

The *Singlaxian Grandeur* stood not far away, and he moseyed on over to it just in time to meet Robin as she came down the ramp. She nodded a greeting at him. "Glad to see you made it."

"Wasn't so sure there for a minute, but we got through thanks to you and Valerie."

Robin waved the dust away from her face. "Cool planet you've brought us to."

Kalan grinned. "It's not much, but if you want the Damu Michezo, this is where you'll find it."

A moment later Valerie, Bob, Flynn, and Garcia joined them outside the ship. Valerie cast a wary eye on the passing crowds. "Tell me about these alien species."

"Sorry to tell you, ma'am," Kalan replied, "but you're the alien here."

There was no humor in her eyes when she replied, "You know what I mean."

Kalan nodded and got to work pointing out the various races of the Vurugu system. "The little guys are the Skulla. They control most of the power in this system."

"What's with all the tattoos?" Robin asked.

"It's a religious thing. Some they get on holy days, and, let me tell you, they've got a lot of holy days. Others signify rank. Some they earn in the fighting pits." He nodded toward a different species. "The big guys that look like they have rocks growing over their skin are Norruls. They're not from this system, but the Skulla ship them in as slaves."

Garcia nodded. "We had a little run-in with one of them earlier. Valerie had to teach him some manners."

Kalan couldn't hide how impressed he was by that. He'd never fought a Norrul, and it wasn't on his to-do list. If Valerie took one of them down, she might have a chance in the Damu Michezo.

"What about those guys with green skin?" Valerie asked. "We saw the hijackers on the ship, but you didn't tell us their race."

"Pallicons," Kalan replied. "Like I mentioned, they're shapeshifters. You'll see some other groups in the fights, but those three comprise the bulk of the combatants."

Kalan noticed that many of the passersby were staring at them, which wasn't surprising. While they saw a lot of different species here, Kalan bet they didn't see many Grayhewn, or many whatever-the-hell Valerie and her friends were either.

There was no need to wonder where the fights were held. The entire crowd pressed in one direction, and they could hear the occasional shouts and cheers of the spectators in the distance. Kalan idly wondered if Esur had made it to the stadium yet. He hoped she was sitting in the stands, having a wonderful time being splattered with blood and brain matter.

He gestured toward the huge spires poking toward the sky in the distance. "Those buildings are the homes of the warlords and the rich. As bad as the poor have it on Tol, it's a mighty nice place to live if you're in charge."

Valerie shook her head in disgust. She put her hands on her hips and looked out over the dusty streets. "Now we just have to figure out how to get me into the fights."

"Ah," Kalan said, suddenly remembering. "I think I can help you there. I made a new friend on the transport, and she gave me the rundown. You have to get one of the warlords to sponsor you. You fight as their representative. If you win you move up in your social standing, but they get a portion of your income for the rest of your life."

"Damn," Bob said. "That's wild. Should be easy enough to find a sponsor, though."

Valerie slowly shook her head. "Maybe not. They don't know me, and having an unknown fight as their representative could make them look weak."

Kalan nodded. "That was the sense I got, too. And there's something else—you won't get in to see a warlord without a letter of introduction. Warlord Nobir runs a tight operation."

"Remind me who that is again?" Valerie requested.

"He controls most of this system," Kalan explained. "Also goes by the name 'the Bandian,' which was apparently some legendary warrior race. He killed the previous leader, guy named Sslake. The people loved Sslake. Hell, I don't give a rotting carcass about politics and even *I* loved him. We elected him and everything, but that little experiment in democracy ended when the Bandian came along and took control."

"Huh," Valerie said. "And the Bandian wouldn't happen to be the guy whose ships I just blew up, would he?"

Kalan smiled. "The very same."

"Wonderful." Valerie thought a moment. "Grayhewn, you said you knew half the scum in the galaxy. Does that mean you know someone who can forge me papers?"

Kalan scratched his head. In theory it was possible. The sabies had an extensive underground network. If there were any sabies on this dried-out husk of a planet, finding a document forger shouldn't be a problem. "I'll do my best."

Valerie looked at him for a long moment. "I need better than your best. I need you to get it done."

He'd worked for too many shady backstabbing bosses, and he appreciated her direct approach. "Yes, ma'am. I'm on it."

## 7

**Planet Tol: Capital Market District**

In the five years since leaving prison, Kalan had only used his saby connections three times. The reason for this was simple: once you started relying on them, it became incredibly difficult to stop. The kids who'd grown up in SEDE took care of each other on the outside, and many of them had gone on to do great things.

The problem was that for sabies "great things" meant "achieved high status in the criminal underworld" and "take care of each other" meant "help each other make connections in the criminal underworld."

Kalan had promised both his mother and himself that he wouldn't go that route. He'd vowed to walk the straight and narrow, and he'd done exactly that. Mostly.

But his employer needed forged papers, so it was time to put those saby connections to work. He pushed his sleeves up to his elbows, revealing the stylized arrow tattoos on his forearms that marked him as a former underage resident of SEDE, and he began to mill about the crowd.

The odds of being randomly spotted by another saby in this crowd were very long indeed, but he didn't need for that to happen. People who ran in shady circles knew that stylized arrow tattoo, and they knew connecting one saby with another often resulted in a nice payday. He needed someone with underworld connections to spot him, and that was exactly what happened.

Within ten minutes a young female approached him, asking if he was looking for some of his people. He said that he was, and she led him across town to the towering, upscale home of an elderly male. The old male thanked the female, slipped her something Kalan didn't see clearly, and sent her on her way. He introduced himself to Kalan as "Duol."

Duol said he'd been out of SEDE for sixty-two years, and he missed it every day. This struck Kalan as more than a little strange. He'd only been out for five and he'd never missed it for a moment, even when his stomach was empty and he thought of the three mildly disgusting meals they provided every day.

It took another hour before the old male agreed to direct Kalan to the best forger in the city. He asked maybe a thousand questions about SEDE first. Did the Yollins still run Cellblock Forty-Seven? Was that one-legged Skulla still alive? Who ran the gambling circuit these days?

Kalan answered these questions as patiently as he could (Yes, no, and a Pallicon named Gling), but he was anxious to be on his way. He didn't know how long this would take, and Valerie didn't seem like the galaxy's most patient boss.

Eventually the old male took him to see the forger, a pretty Skulla female. One look into her striking orange eyes and Kalan began to think maybe facial tattoos were sexy after all.

"I can do what you ask," the forger said, "and I can do it quickly. I have papers that will get you an introduction to a low-level warlord named Palnik. I'll have to make some adjustments. They were made for a female named Marwood, so if they check your friend's DNA, you're dust-choked. But they will pass the automated checks."

"That's wonderful," Kalan said. In truth, he hadn't been sure he'd be able to pull this off when Valerie assigned it to him. Knowing he wouldn't have to go back and face her empty-handed was a huge relief.

The forger shot him a sly smile. "The one thing I never do is work for free. You want the papers? It's going to cost you."

Kalan took a half-step backwards. The way the female was staring at his midsection while she spoke made him more than a little uncomfortable. He exchanged a glance with Duol, who seemed equally bemused by the situation. "Uh, what sort of payment did you have in mind?"

The female paused, then cackled as she realized what he was implying. "I was staring at the Tralen-14 hanging on your hip, you conceited asshole. Hand it over."

A wave of relief washed over Kalan, quickly followed by a sharp pang of indignation. He *really* liked that pistol.

"What's it going to be?" the forger prodded. "Hand over the Tralen, or you'll be walking out of here without any papers. And if your friend tries to approach a warlord without papers, she'll be rotting in the Bandian's prison until he wakes up cranky one morning and decides to use her for target practice."

Kalan would almost like to see the Bandian try. From the little he knew of Valerie, he was fairly certain she wouldn't peacefully allow the guards to take her into custody. Still, he'd been sent here to do a job.

He turned to Duol. "You're sure the papers are good enough to pass inspection?"

The forger answered before the old male could. "The only difference between my papers and the real thing is the validation checks never red-flag mine."

Kalan sighed and set the gun on the table.

So it was that twenty minutes later, Kalan walked out of the forger's home with a freshly minted set of papers and no pistol. It turned out that the term "papers" was figurative; the data was actually stored on a small chip.

"I gotta say, Duol, you came through for me. Thank you."

The old male smiled proudly. "Let it never be said Duol of Tol doesn't live up to obligations to his fellow sabies."

Kalan clapped him on the back. "Hear, hear."

Duol halted mid-step, and Kalan nearly stumbled forward as he too tried to stop. The old man's brow furrowed as he stared at something down the block.

Kalan followed his gaze and saw three strange creatures marching toward a doorway with ancient, peeling green paint. The creatures looked like Skulla, complete with intricate facial tattoos, but they were taller than Kalan and at least as broad. "What the hell are they?"

Duol didn't take his eyes off the men as he answered. "Genetically-modded Skulla. The Bandian is trying to make the perfect Skulla soldiers. You'll see a lot of his failed genetic experiments wandering around this damn planet. Looks like these guys are calling on Nata." He shook his head sadly. "That boy's a damn fool."

Kalan glanced at the impossibly large Skulla and then back at Duol. "Sorry, could you walk that back for me? Who's Nata?"

"A young male running a food station out near the port. He owes Warlord Nibor back tribute."

"Tribute? What's that? Taxes?"

The old male shook his head. "No, he pays his taxes. Tribute is more like extortion. The Bandian's goons charge you a percentage of whatever they think you're earning. In return for paying, they don't kill you and burn down your home."

"Hell of a deal," Kalan said dryly.

"In Nata's case, they vastly overestimated his income. I tried to tell him he had to find some way to come up with the payment, but it looks like he failed."

Kalan drew a deep breath and reminded himself this was none of his business. He'd been sent on a job, and that job had nothing to do with protecting kids who couldn't afford payments to the mob boss running this ass-backward system. His best bet was to keep moving and get back to Valerie as quickly as possible.

But the way those modified Skulla moved, the arrogant way they carried themselves as if the world owed them whatever they felt like taking, reminded Kalan of some of the guards at SEDE—the ones who didn't mind demanding things from the prisoners. Things they had no right to take, like alone-time in dark corners with the female prisoners.

Kalan gritted his teeth at the memory. He felt himself moving forward without even meaning to. His brain hadn't decided what it wanted to do yet, but his feet were intent on enacting justice.

"Kalan," Duol whispered loudly, "what the hell are you doing?"

He ignored it and strode toward the Skulla, earnestly wishing he still had that Tralen-14 on his belt.

The goons stood in front of the green door, and after a moment a young male who had to be Nata opened it. The first guard grabbed him by the throat and roughly pulled him outside.

Nata whimpered in fear as they forced him to his knees and put a pistol to his head.

"We've been patient," the first guard said in an unnaturally deep voice, "but our patience ends here. Now you'll serve as an example."

Kalan reached the rearmost guard and punched him as hard as he could in the back of the head. The Skulla's head rocked forward, but—impossibly—he managed to remain upright. Kalan's hand throbbed with pain, as if he'd punched a brick wall. He ignored it and reached down, pulling the guard's pistol from its holster. Then he wrapped his arm around the guard's neck and put the pistol to his temple.

The other two Skulla turned, and their mouths fell open in surprise when they saw a strange gray alien holding a weapon to their friend's head.

"Nobody move!" Kalan shouted. His eyes flicked to the pistol, and he realized what it was. "Hey, a Tralen-14! I love these things!"

## 8

## Planet Tol: Capital Market District

Kalan didn't give much thought to what he'd done until it was too late. The sun was beating down on him, and he blinked fast to get as much dust as possible out of his eyes.

He held the gun to the head of the heavily-modded seven-foot-tall Skulla in front of him. The other two glared at him like they couldn't believe someone could possibly be so dumb as to challenge them. In that moment, Kalan didn't disagree with their assessment.

He'd attacked three authorities on an alien world where he was supposed to be keeping a low profile. Even if he managed to get out of this, he'd still brought unnecessary attention on himself, and maybe Valerie's team. He silently cursed his stupidity.

And yet he'd done it to protect a kid. If he were being honest, he would admit he'd do the exact same thing one hundred times out of one hundred.

The two other guards exchanged quick glances, then

both started slowly inching away from each other to try to flank him.

"Stop right here, or your friend gets—" That was as far as he made it before the Skulla threw his head back. It painfully connected with Kalan's chin.

Kalan staggered back a step, his grip loosening enough for the Skulla to slip out of it.

The other two quickly spread out and their hands went to their weapons.

Kalan hadn't intended for this to turn into a shootout. He hadn't intended much of anything, but here he was. His enemies were drawing on him, and he had no choice. He raised the Tralen-14 and fired at the guard to his right, dropping him with three quick blasts to the chest.

He turned, intending to fire on the guard to his left, but found the unarmed guard charging him. Instinctively, he moved his aim to that guard and fired at center mass. The big guard tumbled forward and Kalan had to dodge to his left to avoid the body.

"You have any idea what you just did?" the last guard snarled. His gun was trained on Kalan, and Kalan knew there'd be no way he could get a shot off before the guard dropped him.

Thankfully he didn't need to. Nata, the boy they'd come to make an example of, had risen from the dirt and snuck up beside the guard. He threw a wild haymaker of a punch that connected with the big Skulla's left ear. The guard was more surprised than hurt by the blow, but it was enough.

The guard turned an angry face toward Nata, and Kalan was clear to fire. He put two shots into the guard's chest and one in his head for good measure.

Kalan drew a deep breath, the adrenaline still coursing through his body. He scanned the squat, simple homes lining the street and saw more than a few Skulla standing at windows, presumably having watched what just went down.

Someone touched his shoulder and Kalan spun, ready to attack. It was Duol, his face scrunched with concern. "We need to get you the hell out of here *now*."

Nata looked shell-shocked. Kalan wished he had time to stay and talk to the kid, to make sure he was all right, but Duol was correct. They needed to get out of there before more goons arrived.

"Will the kid be okay?" he asked Duol as they wove down the side streets, working their way back toward the old man's home.

Duol nodded. "He's a survivor. If he has any sense—and I think he does—he'll find a friend or relative to hide out with for a few days. Then I'll help him get off this damned ball of dust."

Kalan raised a skeptical eyebrow. "How are you going to do that?"

Duol grinned sheepishly. "Didn't I tell you? I'm in the import-export business."

Kalan knew without asking that Duol meant the illegal kind of import-export. Duol was a smuggler.

Duol sighed. "Warlord Nibor and his damn modded Skulla. Things like that shakedown you just saw are all too common these days. It's not like it was back when Sslake was in charge. Sslake wasn't perfect, but he was the closest thing I've ever seen to an honest politician."

"Now I know you're spinning fairy tales," Kalan said

with a chuckle. The only things he'd ever gotten from politicians were headaches.

"I don't blame you for thinking that, but in Sslake's case it's the truth."

Kalan whistled through his teeth. "Damn. It's a shame he died."

A shadow crossed Duol's face.

"What is it?" Kalan asked.

After a long moment Duol answered, "Nothing."

"That wasn't nothing. I saw your face when I mentioned that Sslake died. You know something."

Duol gave Kalan a hard look before he spoke. "Maybe I do, but it's not the kind of thing you say out in the street. Wait until we get to my house."

They walked another ten minutes in mostly silence, weaving their way through alleys and side streets and avoiding the main roads they'd used on their way to the forger's home.

When they finally reached their destination, Duol led Kalan inside and pulled the curtains shut before resuming the conversation.

Even then he spoke in a low, conspiratorial tone. "Not many people know this. I wouldn't tell it to anyone, not even another saby. But after what you did for that kid, dumb as it was, I'm going to tell you."

Kalan waited, afraid to speak for fear that he might say the wrong thing and discourage the old male from continuing.

Duol drew a deep breath. "Sslake isn't dead."

Kalan tilted his head. "Where the hell is he?"

"A place you and I know all too well," he said with a

smile. "I don't know why the Bandian kept him alive. Maybe he's trying to get Sslake to support him, or maybe he's going to use him as some sort of bargaining chip. All I know is, the Bandian didn't kill Sslake. He abducted him and shipped him to SEDE."

It took a moment for that information to sink into Kalan's brain. "Wait, SEDE? *Our* SEDE?"

Duol nodded. "The isolation block, from what I hear. It's a damn shame. He was one of the good ones, and you and I both know what that place can do to good people."

"Yeah. It chews on them until they aren't so good anymore. But wait, how do you know this?"

The old male smiled wryly. "I made friends with the pilots who run the transport ships."

Kalan's eyes narrowed. That was impossible. One of the things that made SEDE the most secure prison in the galaxy was that it was constantly on the move. It was hard to arrange a breakout if you didn't know where the damn ship was at any given moment. Even the movement of the transport ships that carried new inmates to and paroled inmates off SEDE was a closely-guarded secret.

Or so Kalan had thought.

Duol continued, "A lot of folks don't have anywhere to go when they get out of SEDE, so the transport pilots came to an arrangement with the Bandian. They bring those people here to Tol, to be used as slaves or as fodder for the lowest-level fights. Not the Damu Michezo, but the under-ground stuff."

"You're kidding me." The very thought of it made Kalan simmer with rage. To finally get out of that hell-hole, thinking you have a new start—a chance to make things right—only to be sold into a brand-new form of hell.

"I'm afraid I'm not."

Kalan glared at Duol. "Let me guess—you pay those same pilots to smuggle contraband to SEDE?"

The old male turned his palms upward with an innocent look on his face. "A Skulla has to make a living."

Kalan couldn't blame Duol too much, even though he was working with despicable people. During Kalan's childhood on SEDE, the contraband had been one of the few things that always brought him a job.

The screen on the wall chirped, startling Kalan.

"What's that chirp mean?" he asked.

"City-wide alert." Duol marched to the screen and tapped it a few times. "Holy tongue dust, this isn't good."

Kalan's pulse quickened as he began to suspect the cause of the alert. "What is it?"

"Seems a big gray alien killed some of Warlord Nibor's loyal soldiers today. Luckily, a few helpful citizens managed to grab a picture of him through their windows." He turned toward Kalan and gave him a joyless grin. "Congratulations. You're now officially the most wanted being on Tol."

## 9

## Planet Tol: The Slums

While Kalan was out working to get her the letter of introduction needed for the fights, Valerie and the team decided to check out one of the Skulla bars their companions from the journey here had told them was a must.

Little did Valerie know that the Skulla idea of a bar was more akin to a fight club. As soon as they walked into the little building they were surrounded by crude carvings on the walls of people fighting in a great arena, and alien scratches along the walls that must've been their alphabet. It smelled of sweat and blood, the call of bloodlust loud below it all.

When Valerie stepped off the last step she noted it was as they had figured—male and female Skulla lounging around the place, drinking and talking, two in a corner rubbing hands in a very awkward and seemingly inappropriate way. But in the middle of it all, where a ring of them had gathered, two fighters were beating the shit out of each other.

"We shouldn't stop it, should we?" Flynn asked. "I mean, they're all here for this, right?"

"Try and stop it," the Skulla at the next table said. "That would be the funniest thing I've seen all week, and I saw an Orduan try to eat a Woro earlier today."

"And that's funny?" Valerie asked, not sure if she should ignore the guy.

"Hilarious! You see what we're up against here. Go for it —intervene."

Valerie and the others glanced at the female Skulla serving drinks, then meandered over.

"How many drinks if the scrawny one wins a fight?" Valerie said, motioning to Robin.

"Wait a minute!" Robin protested, but the bartender was already smiling.

"I pick? A round on the house." The bartender leaned back, poured a shot, and slid it over. It was green with a line of red down the middle, resembling a snake's eye. "First one on me, to calm the nerves."

"No nerves needing calming here," Robin said, waving her off. "Where do I sign up?"

There was a loud crash and they all spun to see that the larger of the two fighters had been slammed into a table. His back had shattered it, and he lay groaning on the floor.

"Winner!" a tall Skulla said, raising the other fighter's hand in the air. When the bartender went over and whispered something in her ear, the female looked at Robin suspiciously.

"You sure we should be doing this?" Robin hissed at Valerie. "Seems like playing, when—"

"Wrong," Valerie interrupted. "We're not playing. We're getting in with the locals, seeing what they're really like. Seeing if we can earn some trust, maybe make a friend."

"By me beating the snot out of some guy?"

Valerie shrugged. "Maybe? Or maybe it's better if you don't whup him too hard. Make it look like beginner's luck."

"Wonderful."

The announcer turned to the patrons of the bar and smiled, arms spread. "My fellow miscreants, do we have a treat for you! For the first time in Tol history, we have a special treat. A *human* fighter!"

She gestured to Robin and everyone cheered, though half seemed to think it was some sort of joke.

"And why aren't *you* doing it?" Robin asked Valerie as she nodded to the room.

"Can't give up the moves yet, and can't let myself get out of control."

Robin sighed and stepped forward, hand raised.

"And her opponent tonight will be… Volunteers?"

Several large men stepped forward, but a pair of female twins shoved the others out of the way. They only came up to Robin's chest, and glared at her like they would eat her for lunch.

"The champions have been chosen!" the announcer stated, stepping back and raising a fist. "Fight!"

"She acts like it's the damned arena in here," Valerie heard someone behind her whisper to his friend. "Give me a break."

Valerie glanced back to see two Skulla at the bar, a male and female of similar look and build. They might have been brother and sister, or—and Valerie hated to admit this to herself—it might've been that she still couldn't tell them apart so well.

CRACK!

The sound drew her attention back to the fight, where Robin had apparently served one of the twins with a knee to the face. The former vampire stepped back, releasing the head to allow the unconscious Skulla to collapse to the floor.

One of them out, just like that. The crowd was stunned. Silence followed, then the other gave a blood-curdling scream and charged Robin. This one was either more skilled or not overconfident, because she was smart enough to stop out of Robin's range before leaping for her legs.

Robin kicked the Skulla, catching her in the ribs, but the Skulla still managed to grab her other leg, taking Robin down.

It was about time, too, because Robin was making this look *way* too easy.

Now that they were grappling, the Skulla attempting to rain blows on her opponent. The attacks kept coming, but Robin cast a quick smile Valerie's way—fast enough that the rest of them likely didn't notice.

An elbow connected, and blood splattered from Robin's lip. She snarled, grabbed the twin by the shirt, and tossed her head-first into the closest wall.

The Skulla pushed herself up and staggered toward Robin, but the woman apparently couldn't help herself—

she ran forward, swept the Skulla's legs, and leaped into the air to land a sound kick to her head before the Skulla had even hit the ground.

It was definitely over.

No cheering this time, Valerie noted. Some grumbling, some confusion, and many glares.

"A deal's a deal," the bartender said, pouring several more drinks for them. With a wave of her hand to some nearby tough-guy Skulla, she added, "Get those losers out of my bar."

The tough guys dragged the twins out while Valerie and her team went for the drinks, not sure what to make of this situation. It certainly hadn't gone as she'd expected. And then it hit her—of *course* you don't show up in some foreign place and kick their asses. This was different from the arena. A glance around showed very proud Skulla, many glancing at her from the corners of their eyes.

"You didn't give them a chance," she hissed at Robin as she walked back over and downed her drink.

Robin wiped blood from her lip and shrugged. "I know how to win, not lose. You want that, you put Bob in the next fight."

"Hey, now," Bob protested. "You don't know what I'm capable of. I've modified myself in more than one way, if you get my drift. Fighting, fu—"

"Nobody gives a shit, Bob," Robin countered, then took Valerie's drink and downed that too. "That's for making me hurt people. Or…Skulla."

"You don't think I'll be doing my fair share of that in the contest?" Valerie asked. "Hell, by that logic I'd be stumbling back to the ship wasted tonight."

Strange thuds came from out back, then more, followed by a yelp. A *crack* followed, and some of the Skulla started trickling out through the rear door.

"What's that about?" Valerie wondered aloud.

"Justice," the Skulla brother from the bar said. "Or that's what they call it."

"Watch yourself," the bartender warned the brother.

He tilted his head back and forth. "They lost, they get punished. I understand it, but that doesn't mean I like it."

Valerie didn't wait to ask what that meant. She had already been heading for the door.

"Here we go," Garcia said behind her. "Look lively."

They all followed, with a groan from Bob.

As Valerie had expected, the twins had been pinned against a wall as several of the tough guys, and others, too, took turns hitting them with batons—long and metal, with a glowing red line up the side. Each hit made the red glow brighter, as if charging it.

The bartender joined them now, standing beside Valerie. "Best go back inside, *Wandrei*."

"*Wandrei*?" Valerie asked, debating her move here. Dammit, this was *her* fault, but intervening would make enemies fast—which was counterproductive to her mission.

"'Outsider,' is an easier way to say it," the bartender replied. "Your translator chip pick that one up?"

Valerie glanced at him and frowned, then moved in to stop the beating. Screw it, she was a *Wandrei*, right? So what would hold her back from stopping this brutality? This wasn't justice. It was barbaric.

The first tough guy turned on her and tried to hit her

with the baton. She grabbed it mid-strike, twisted it from his hand, and tossed it over her shoulder to clatter against a couple trash bins.

"Who do you think you are?" a larger one said, clearly modified for size. He attempted to grab her, while the first one came in with a fist.

She stepped back and slammed their heads together, then did it again when she saw that it hadn't had much of an effect. Those two dropped, groaning, and three more took their place.

By this point Robin and the rest of the Elites were at her side, and there was a clear standoff. Everyone out here —and there were a lot of them now—had seen what Robin could do. Now they had seen Valerie take on two of their thugs. None were eager to make the first move.

"We may be outsiders," Valerie announced, "and this might be a cultural thing we're not supposed to mess with —hitting females in alleys, with metal rods no less. Maybe I'm supposed to walk away, to ignore it? Join in? Well, fuck all of that."

The crowd went from hostile to hostile-and-very-confused.

"You're a nutcase," the bartender said. "You want to do what? Sex with all of what?"

Valerie was so pissed at the situation that she was surprised at her urge to laugh. It hadn't processed that swearing might produce the wrong translation. Either theirs wasn't up to date, or it didn't include curse words.

"Ignore that. Bad translation." She turned to one of the tough guys who was inching toward her. "The point is, we won't just sit by and watch this. They lost, so get over it."

"They humiliated us," the bartender said. "Losing to *Wandrei*. It's our right to take their lives if we want to."

"And if they'd won?"

The bartender simply frowned, not responding, but finally she sniffed the air and smiled. "Anyone else smell a warlord nearby? Maybe we go find us one, tell him what this *Wandrei* did. See how they deal with rulebreakers."

"You're telling me this action is sanctioned?" Valerie scoffed. "An actual rule? If you lose to outsiders, you get torn up in an alley?"

The bartender nodded. "And you're obstructing justice."

"This place is royally fucked-up," Bob said under his breath.

"He's right, Val," Garcia chimed in. "Let's roll."

"Listen to your friends," the bartender said, "while you still have a chance."

Valerie wasn't big on being threatened, but right now she was keenly aware of the mission and what becoming Tol's most wanted *Wandrei* might mean.

"We're leaving," Valerie said, ignoring the hushed protests from Robin and Flynn, who both apparently wanted to tear the tough guys new assholes. "But I have a feeling we'll be seeing more of each other."

The tough guys were glancing at the bartender as if waiting for the word to pounce, but the bartender strode back into the bar. After a moment of confusion, the others started following.

"Come on," Valerie said. "We've seen enough of this shit show for now. Let's find Kalan and see if he got what we need."

**Planet Tol: Capital Market District**

Despite Duol's best attempts to talk him out of it, Kalan wanted to get back to Valerie as quickly as possible.

Duol argued—probably wisely— that he should stay off the streets. From the alert, it appeared that only Kalan had been photographed. Duol had been uninvolved enough that no one thought to snap a picture of him. For that, Kalan was grateful. It was stupid enough that he'd gotten involved himself. He was glad he hadn't gotten this old male in trouble, especially after he'd been so helpful.

Kalan said his goodbyes to Duol and slipped out the door, heading back toward the ship. He tried to raise Valerie on the communicator as he walked, but she didn't answer. He hoped his antics hadn't caused her trouble. It was all too possible someone might have seen them together in the spaceport.

He was almost to the ship when his communicator chirped and he heard Valerie's voice on the other end. She sounded about as stressed as he felt, and she gave him a new location to meet, a bit south of the spaceport.

As he walked, Kalan stayed alert for the presence of any authorities, but his gaze kept drifting to the skyline. There he could see the twisting spires of the homes of the rich, far from the dusty streets where the poor wallowed. Just more evidence that things were messed up here on Tol, and in the Vurugu system as a whole.

When he reached the meeting place, he looked around. Plenty of people were milling past, but he didn't see Valerie or her crew among them. Then he spotted a shoulder sticking out of the shadows of an alley off the main thoroughfare. Creeping closer, he squinted at the figure.

"Bob? Is that you?" he asked.

The beady-eyed man stuck his head out of the alley and angrily motioned for Kalan to join him.

He ducked into the alley and found Valerie and her crew lurking in the shadows.

Robin frowned at him. "Subtlety certainly isn't your strong suit. We've been on this planet, what? A couple hours?"

Kalan sighed. "So you've heard about the alert?"

"They were playing it over speakers in the street," Flynn informed him.

"Wonderful." He turned toward Valerie. "How about you lot? Any trouble?"

Valerie grimaced. "You don't want to know, and I don't have time to explain it anyway. You get the letter of introduction?"

Kalan nodded and handed her the chip, explaining a little about its usage. "It's as legit as possible, but it contains the DNA of this Marwood woman. If the warlord checks yours against it…"

"It'll get us through the door," Valerie replied. "That's enough." She shook her head in disgust. "This planet needs us."

"That's why we're here," Robin reminded her. "To bring them some Earth-style justice."

Kalan didn't even bother asking what that meant.

Bob scratched at his head. "I don't know. So we take out some warlord, what then? Another takes his place?"

The words reminded Kalan of what Duol had told him, and he looked at Valerie. "You know Sslake, that leader I told you about? The one the people loved?"

"Yeah, what about him?"

"Turns out he's not dead. They're holding him in SEDE."

"The prison you grew up in," Valerie confirmed.

Kalan nodded.

"Damn," Bob exclaimed. "Somebody should bust him out of there. Maybe he'd be open to working with—" He stopped, catching himself, and glanced at Kalan. "Well, he'd be better than this Bandian guy. That's all I'm saying."

"Nice idea, but we have our hands plenty full taking out this asshole warlord," Valerie said.

"I don't." The words were out of Kalan's mouth before he knew he was going to speak. They sounded insane, even to him, but something about them felt right. After the little things he'd seen so far on this planet and the things he'd heard about this Sslake guy, he believed that something had to be done.

Valerie raised an eyebrow. "Are you really saying you're

willing to break into SEDE to rescue this political prisoner?"

Kalan smiled, hoping they didn't see through his bravado. "I'm willing to try. Look, I know the prison, and I know the prisoners. I think I even know a way to get there. And I'm a wanted man, so I need to get the hell off this planet anyway. Every leader I've ever known wasn't worth their title. If this guy is... Well, I need to see that for myself."

Valerie nodded, a smile slowly creeping onto her face. "Then I guess you'd better know who you're doing it for. My crew and I work for the Etheric Federation."

He drew a sharp breath. "I should have known."

"You got a problem with that?"

In truth, he didn't know much about the Etheric Federation. Just rumors. Some said they were in expansion mode, trying to force their way of life on every planet in the galaxy. Others said they were heroes, bringing freedom and justice everywhere they went. Kalan didn't know enough to have an opinion.

He met Valerie's gaze. "I don't have a problem with it. If you're going to take down the Bandian and restore Sslake to power, that's all I need to know."

"Good." Valerie turned to Bob. "You're going with Kalan."

The man went pale. "Wait, what?"

Robin grinned. "It was sort of your idea. You said we needed someone to take the Bandian's place, right?"

"I didn't mean..." Bob stammered. "All I was trying to say was..."

Kalan held up a hand. "This really isn't necessary."

"Actually it is," Valerie said firmly. "I know he's a pain in the ass, but Bob's good with the high-tech stuff. And I get the feeling you're not."

"Very much not," Kalan admitted. He knew the physical components of engines, and could replace just about any part, but when it came to programming, he was lost.

"Then it's settled. You two go rescue this Sslake guy from space prison while we take down the most powerful warlord in the system."

"Man, we have the best jobs!" Garcia said.

Kalan nodded along with the others, but in his head he was wondering what kind of crazies he'd signed on with. If this was their idea of fun, he didn't want to see what they considered stressful.

Valerie stepped up to Kalan and put a hand on his arm. "I know we haven't known each other long, and I appreciate that you're willing to do this. It shows me what kind of person you are."

He shrugged, trying to hide his blush. In truth, he didn't consider himself all that good of a person. He did what he needed to do to survive. And yeah, if he came across someone who needed help he gave them a hand, but it was nothing more than that. "You're giving me too much credit. I'm just a guy with a special knowledge of the prison who has nothing better to do."

Valerie looked him in the eye, her expression dead serious. "Maybe this will help you realize you're more than that." She turned to Bob and clapped on him the back. "Bob, you're... You're all right too."

Bob grinned like he'd been paid the highest compliment in the world.

Kalan chuckled. "All right, Bob. Let's see about catching a transport to SEDE."

"And how the hell are we going to do that?" he asked, his voice edgy with concern.

"I can't believe I'm saying this," Kalan said, "but I know a guy."

**Planet Tol**

Valerie watched Kalan go, knowing a lot of this mission now rested on his shoulders. She was all about trusting others, but considering that she had just met him and that he could end up dead as easily as he could succeed, she felt a twinge of worry.

If that happened she'd never forgive herself, even though she knew there was nothing she could do. As for the mission at hand, she supposed her only move at that point would be to storm in and kick everyone's ass until she got answers. Seeing as that wouldn't help win these planets to the side of the Etheric Federation in the slightest, she did her best to push those thoughts from her mind and focus on the task before her.

She had her papers and her point of contact. Now all she had to do was meet up with him and see what was needed of her, what her payment would be.

Get it done and earn her way into the fighting contest. Easy enough.

"Proceed with caution, and be ready in case there's trouble," Valerie told Garcia and Flynn.

"This is some kind of shore-duty bull," Flynn asked with a laugh. "Any of you find locals who want a real man, you send them my way."

Robin smiled and shrugged. At Valerie's glance she said, "What? The idea of him with one of those short Skulla females is kinda funny."

"Don't encourage the man," Valerie replied.

"Check back in so we know there's not trouble," Garcia said. "I'm not going to sit around all day with my fingers crossed, wondering what happened to you."

Valerie nodded, then wished them luck and nodded to Robin. Soon they were making their way back to the city and its vast spread of rundown shacks on this side, tall mansions and the like on the other.

"There," Robin stated, pointing to a large building that reminded Valerie of the arena where she had first found Robin. While that one had been in ruins, although partially rebuilt to function as the headquarters to the assassins who had trained her, this one had a smooth, gleaming surface that looked to be somewhere between metal and rock. Pillars anchored cloth that provided shade for viewers, and outside were massive statues of various monsters with sharp teeth, wings, and in one case tentacles.

"Please tell me those are statues of mythical creatures and not some alien species," Valerie said. "I don't need my dreams going crazy on me."

"You and me both," Robin replied.

They worked their way around the place to a spot on a nearby hill that overlooked the arena, ignoring the several Skulla who glanced at them with curiosity as they passed. Already males and females were in there training. Some of the less-modified, clearly poorer-class fighters were training in one corner, and a large warrior watched, amused, from the stands.

"This is where we'll find the warlord," Valerie said, not liking it already. She glared as they headed to the rear of the arena, where several subservient-looking Skulla lurked.

What sort of civilization made people fight to the death? The way she understood it, outsiders gained a chance at joining society by entering the fights. Skulla, locals, and those who were already part of Tol's society could fight to earn their way up in the social system, but the price of defeat was death.

As far as she was concerned it didn't make sense that anyone would fight. However, people got desperate. On top of that, Kalan had told her there was a whole pyramid scheme going on. Warlords would put a person up for a fight and if that person won, the warlord would get a cut of their future income. Then this victor might get their own person, a lowlander who would fight and give them a percentage, and part of that would then be paid to the first warlord.

It was a complicated system, one Valerie detested even before having to fight and possibly kill anyone.

But she had her orders.

The two of them reached a wall that was mostly rubble and approached the nearest Skulla, a female with spiral tattoos like wind.

"We're looking for Warlord Palnik," Valerie stated, flashing her forged chip, hoping that would be enough.

The Skulla looked at her, frowned, and nodded to the group behind her. "They're his, over there. Don't be flashing papers quite yet though, or someone will take them."

Valerie nodded and was about to go when the Skulla held out a hand. "You one of those Federation types? We've heard about you."

"What've you heard?" Robin interjected.

"The big shots warn against you." The Skulla glanced around nervously. "Say you are trying to take over the universe. Well, I say *good*—hit them where it hurts. I seriously doubt anyone's as bad as our current system."

"Is that right?" Valerie pursed her lips in thought, wondering how many other Skulla felt this way.

"The name's Orane. You know...if you survive long enough to make a difference here."

"I don't plan on dying," Valerie replied, "if that's what you mean."

"You have the papers, you're looking for Warlord Palnik... Certainly sounds like you're looking to die. You're going to fight in the Damu Michezo. Just know that whatever crazy warriors you had back on your planet, you're going to need to multiply that times a billion in craziness here. So, as I said, *if* you survive and really plan on making a difference, look me up."

"Thanks," Valerie said, not sure how to take that interaction. She nodded to Robin and the two meandered over to the other group, careful to keep the papers out of sight this time.

A clearly modified Skulla with arms thicker than seemed natural was showing an odd version of a bow and arrow to his buddies. It was made of a pure white wood, and the arrow was crafted from an orange metal.

"This little fart-sucker will blow out a wall," the Skulla said, pulling back on the arrow. "Take down the wall, then just send in the guns. Easy. As. *That*." On the last word he let the arrow fly, and it hit an old vessel that looked very similar to the antigrav Pods Valerie was used to back home.

The vehicle exploded into a ball of flames.

"Ten thousand snits," the Skulla said, beaming until he noticed Valerie and Robin. "Oh hell no, what the hell are you supposed to be? Talk about ugly! I didn't know they made them that tall."

Valerie tried not to laugh, considering that this Skulla resembled a tatted-up prune. His forehead folded in wrinkles, one eye was clearly larger than the other, and the thick arms made him look way off-balance. Maybe this was what the locals found attractive?

"I'm told you're affiliated with Warlord Palnik," Valerie stated, standing tall with her thumbs tucked into her pants.

The Skulla glanced between her and his buddies, who were starting to back away.

"No, wait..." he started, but they broke for it—all but an especially short one with fewer tattoos than the rest. The first Skulla turned back to her and glared. "You owe me ten thousand snits."

"I have no idea what a snit is, nor any intention of paying you," Valerie replied.

"You are looking at the next champion of the Damu Michezo," Robin interjected, gesturing to Valerie as a priest would a god. "They will call her amazing, but you can call her 'Valerie.'"

The Skulla furrowed his thin brow. "Is this some sort of routine you two—whatever you are—do? Listen, the only reason you're still alive is because you mentioned my master's name. If you owe him money and he found out I was the one who took it or killed the chance at regaining it... Well, that wouldn't be good. So talk. Do you owe him money?"

"I'm here to speak with him."

The Skulla stared. When neither Valerie nor Robin spoke for a few beats, he started laughing. "You're either the toughest little wolo this side of Aranch or just plain stupid. Which is it?"

"Why don't you try her and find out?" Robin offered.

"*Thanks,*" Valerie said, turning to her friend and not even trying to hide her irritation. As she turned back to the Skulla a fist slammed into her jaw, knocking her backward.

This little bastard was strong!

"Come on, then," the Skulla said, setting aside his bow and arrow. A couple of the others moved in to watch.

"I'm here to speak with Palnik," Valerie hissed, "not humor you with some street brawl."

"A little demonstration of good faith," the Skulla replied. "Show me what you're made of, so I know you're worth my time."

Again he moved to attack, but this time Valerie used one of the techniques Garcia had shown her, simply side-stepping and grabbing the little male from behind, lever-aging his momentum to flip him onto his back.

"We done here?" she asked, pinning his chest with one of her boots.

"Hardly," he growled, then swept her leg with his massive arm and rolled over to pounce.

"Tell me, what's your name? I want to be able to tell Palnik who I killed to get to him. I have a feeling he'll thank me as he pisses on your grave."

"Korak," the Skulla replied, baring his teeth. "And I don't know what a grave is. Might want to get your translator fixed, or just shut your trap and take this beating I'm about to dole out."

She'd had enough, and was about to show this guy what she was made of when his eyes went large and his jaw dropped. He stared beyond her.

"You jackass-faced wolo chompter," he screamed, and charged right past her.

One of the other Skulla had used the opportunity to steal Korak's bow and arrows.

A glance at Robin showed that she was pursing her lips with a raised eyebrow, likely having the same thought as Valerie. Opportunity had struck!

"Let's get him," Valerie shouted, taking off after the thief.

---

**Planet Tol: Capital Spaceport**

Kalan and Bob waited on the dusty platform as Duol had instructed them to do.

The old male had been surprised when Kalan had showed up again so soon after leaving, but he'd agreed to help them. Thankfully with the large crowds on Tol for the Damu Michezo there was a high demand for lower-level fights, which meant the transport pilots from SEDE were dropping off newly-released convicts on an almost daily basis.

Duol had quickly made arrangements, and they'd only had to wait a few hours before leaving to meet with the transport pilot on this anonymous platform in the shadier section of the spaceport.

They'd been standing there about twenty minutes when a scowling Pallicon arrived and grabbed them both by the arms.

"What in the dust-tongued hell are you fools doing out in the open?" he growled.

"We were told to wait here," Bob indignantly answered.

Kalan didn't bother speaking. He knew this pilot's type. He was looking for something to bark at them about as a way to establish his dominance. If it hadn't been about their location it would have been about how they were dressed, or how they wore their hair, or some other made-up grievance.

The pilot whirled on Bob. "I don't give a yanecat's ass what you were told! We're on *my* platform, which means we're practically on *my* ship. Which means *my* orders are the only ones that matter here."

Kalan grimaced, trying not to think about the fact that this male was a slaver and a smuggler. Duol was a smuggler too, but at least he smuggled contraband *onto* SEDE. That improved the inmates' lives, at least theoretically. Well, if you didn't take into consideration the prison gangs that controlled the contraband. That was a gray area Kalan didn't want to think about now.

But this Pallicon was something different. He sold living beings. He may have sold people Kalan knew. He may have sold *Julla*.

He pushed the thought away. This guy was his only way aboard SEDE. If he thought too much about the pilot's crimes he'd end up bashing his head in, and then where would he be? Stranded on this dusty fighting-pit of a planet, that's where.

If he wanted to rescue Sslake he needed this ride, so he kept his mouth shut and silently promised himself he'd someday pay this Pallicon a visit and set things right.

The pilot didn't offer his name or any other form of pleasantry, just led them aboard the small but modern transport.

"You'll ride back there," he said, gesturing to the cargo hold, where a handful of small jump seats were bolted to the wall. A grated door with a heavy-duty lock stood between the cockpit and the cargo hold. "I'll leave this door open for now, but if you cause any trouble—"

"We won't," Kalan interjected.

"Good. See that you don't. There are some prison jumpsuits back there left by the prisoners I dropped off on Tol. They aren't clean, but you'll need them if you want to sneak aboard." With that he marched to the cockpit, leaving them alone with the crates in the cargo hold.

Kalan and Bob spent the next few minutes digging through the smelly pile of old uniforms in the corner of the cargo hold. Bob found one right away, but it took Kalan longer to locate one he could squeeze into while still being able to breath.

Once he was dressed, Kalan stared at the seat that was much too small for his bulky form, sighed, and then did his best to sit in it.

Bob took a seat across from him. "Man, that pilot guy's a real asshole, huh?"

"I can hear you." The pilot's tinny voice came through the small speaker mounted on the wall next to Bob's head.

Bob started and let out a high-pitched squeak.

Kalan shook his head sadly at the stupidity of his new partner.

"Ah, good," Bob said, obviously trying to regain a bit of

his composure. "That was a joke. You were meant to hear it."

The pilot's howl of laughter blasted through the tinny speaker. "Sure, and my wife loves that I only send her half my wages."

Kalan was starting to get annoyed with the pilot. He turned toward the speaker. "So where's SEDE flying right now?"

There was a pause, then the pilot said, "Sorry, how's that any of your business?"

Kalan drew a deep breath and forced himself to remain calm. "I only asked because I was wondering how long our flight would be." Depending on the prison's location in the system their journey could be anywhere from a few hours to a few weeks, even if this little transport *was* as powerful as it looked.

The pilot cackled again. "The cargo doesn't get to know the flight plan. We'll get there when we get there."

"I rest my case about him being an asshole," Bob muttered under his breath.

"Heard that, too!" the pilot quickly shot back. "I've got that cargo hold so miked-up you won't be able to fart without me knowing about it."

Neither Kalan nor Bob bothered responding to that.

If Kalan had to guess, he'd say SEDE was relatively close to Tol. From what the old smuggler had said, the Damu Michezo was an especially profitable time to transport ex-cons to Tol, and Kalan would be shocked if SEDE's navigator wasn't in on the scheme, taking a cut of this asshole pilot's profits.

Still, the question was *how* close. The Vurugu system was a damn big place.

A few minutes later the pilot spoke again. "By the way, my bosses on SEDE know I run some contraband, but they aren't aware I'm bringing living cargo this time. If they found out it would be my job, so when they catch you, come up with some other story about how you got aboard."

Kalan had no idea what other plausible explanation they could possibly offer. Besides, if they *were* caught they'd have much bigger concerns than protecting this jerkoff pilot. "Of course. We'd never rat on you."

"Good." There was a long silence before he continued, "I've heard of people wanting to break out of prison, but never someone wanting to break in. What's so important on SEDE?"

"Sorry, but our driver doesn't get to know our plans." The words were out of Kalan's mouth before he could stop them. He knew it was in his best interests to stay on this pilot's good side, but sometimes he couldn't help himself.

"Fine," the pilot barked. "That's what I get for being friendly. You both sit back there and think about the hell you're about to walk into. I saw your tats, big guy, so I know you're a saby. But I'll bet your strange-looking friend there doesn't have a clue what SEDE's like."

"Don't worry about me," Bob said with forced bravado. "I'll be fine."

The pilot chuckled. "Sure you will. Hey, big guy, did you tell him about the Shimmers?"

Bob raised a curious eyebrow.

Kalan sighed, but figured he was going to have to prep

Bob at some point. Now was as good a time as any. "The Shimmers are the guards."

"Yeah?" Bob asked, his voice strained with concern. "What do they look like? Are they big?"

The pilot bellowed with laughter, and Bob scowled at the speaker.

Kalan considered how best to explain the Shimmers. They'd always been part of his life. He'd always known they were there, so they'd seemed normal, but he could see how they might seem bizarre to someone who hadn't grown up in his situation.

"Here's the thing... Shimmers aren't exactly like you and me. They're not made of..." He gestured to Bob's arm.

"Awesome muscle?" Bob asked.

"Um, no. They're not made of flesh. You can't see them. You can't hear them."

Bob went pale, and when he spoke again it was in a hushed tone. "They're ghosts?"

The pilot cackled again.

"No!" Kalan tried to think how to better explain it. "Whatever they're made of is not visible to us, but they can see and hear us fine. If they really concentrate they can make themselves vaguely visible, but all that shows up is a bit of wavering light. Hence their name."

"The Shimmers," Bob repeated weakly.

"As you might imagine, they make pretty great prison guards. You never know where they are, or if they're watching. Usually the first sign you have that they're standing there is a smack upside the head. Then maybe you get a note later officially informing you what you did wrong."

"So let me get this straight," Bob said. "We're breaking into a prison staffed by invisible guards?"

"Invisible, silent, and strong as hell," Kalan confirmed.

"Thanks a lot, Valerie," Bob muttered.

Kalan felt a little sorry for the guy. He'd been in the Vurugu system what, a couple days? And now he was headed straight for the worst place in the system.

He leaned forward. "I'm glad she assigned you and not one of those other guys. Garcia? Flynn? Robin? No thanks. I'd take you any day over those amateurs."

Bob's eyes brightened a little at that. "Really?"

"Of course."

In reality, Bob would have been his last pick by a wide margin. If he'd had the option of selecting a squealing infant or Bob for this task he would have had to think long and hard before making the decision, but Bob needed a confidence boost right now.

"Thanks." Bob leaned back, resting his head on the bulkhead behind him. "That means a lot. Maybe when we get back, we can tell Valerie we'd like to be paired up more often. Maybe we could even become official partners."

Kalan forced a smile onto his face. "Let's not get ahead of ourselves. For now, what do you say we try to get some rest? We'll need to be at our best on SEDE."

"Yeah, you will," the pilot said through the speaker. "By the way, if by some miracle you survive and accomplish whatever shady operation you have going, you'll have to find your own ride home. I was only contracted to take you *to* SEDE. This was a one-way ticket."

## Planet Tol: The Slums

This Skulla thief must've had enhanced legs, because he was running like the wind. Valerie pushed herself faster, not quite going full vampire speed but fast enough to close the gap. She passed Korak as they rounded a series of small huts made of what looked like abalone, though that didn't make sense. The thief dove between a metal craft and an overturned cart of local produce, then leaped to a window sill and jumped from it to a nearby roof.

"I get it back, you take me to Palnik," Valerie demanded, running at Korak's side. His mismatched upper body was slowing him down, and he looked like he was about to vomit.

"Stop that bastard!"

"Say it!"

He grunted, came to a stop, and nodded between wheezing breaths. "Yes, yes, of course."

"Deal," she replied, then turned to Robin. "Don't let him out of your sight."

Robin nodded and Valerie took off after the thief, leaping from the cart to pursue him on the rooftops. Nobody could see her up here, which meant she didn't have to worry about using vampire speed.

No longer holding back, she darted across the rooftop and came down hard on the thief as he tossed the bow to a companion in a window of the next building over. The arrows he was carrying fell, one going over and exploding.

Valerie cursed, leaping down to follow the arrow. The wall of the next building had been blown open, and the female Skulla with the bow was standing there with her mouth open at the sight.

"I'll take that," Valerie said, strolling up to her and snatching it out of her hands. The Skulla glared at her and then ran. The one on the roof took off after her, leaving the arrows where they had fallen.

Good riddance.

There was a loud *screech* and then a metal craft pulled up—apparently law-enforcement Skulla, judging by the vehicle and the uniforms they wore. She was usually on the side of the law but Valerie wasn't sure how it all worked here, so she backed into the shadows.

"Damn feuds," she heard one of them say. "Somebody's going to pay for this."

"Right. Us, if we don't find out who did it," the other replied.

Valerie decided being caught here with this bow wouldn't make the best first impression with local authorities. She pulled the bow over her shoulders and quickly made for the back, then climbed out of the window to come face to face with a large hairy local.

She opened her mouth to explain herself, but its eyes moved to some produce on the ground—a strange looking purple fruit—and it knelt to eat it. The creature was something like a cross between a chimpanzee and a horse, not that she'd seen many of either in her lifetime outside of pictures.

She heard voices from the other side of the house so she took off, grabbing a cloth from the many that had been hung to dry between huts. She wrapped it around her face and head, hoping that would keep her from later being recognized.

Considering that she was by Skulla standards quite tall and easily identified in silhouette, it was a long shot. She would have to ensure nobody saw her. Nobody, that is, but the strange hairy creature. Even so, she took the time to sweep back around and grab the arrows.

Once she reached the rooftop she heard the enforcement officers harassing someone, accusing them of the explosion.

She could either let it go, or do something about it. Of course, there wasn't really a choice. She quickly nocked one of the arrows, not quite sure how to use one of these things, and took aim. The arrow wobbled as it flew but still managed to make contact with the enforcement vehicle, flipping it before sending it into a brick wall nearby.

Curses came from below, and she took off.

Did she feel great about damaging government property? No, especially since part of her mission here was to get in good with the government and find out what it would take to get them to ally with the Etheric Federation.

But she couldn't let some kid take the blame for what had clearly not been his fault. At least no one had been hurt or killed, and the vehicle might have flipped. Maybe it would need a couple dents taken out, at worst.

Korak was looking around frantically, and he spotted Valerie walking up with his bow and explosive arrows.

"You actually did it," he announced, mouth agape. He held out his hand to accept his gear, but she hesitated.

"Impressed?"

He nodded. "Enough so that if you stop stalling I'll take you to meet my master right now. And enough that if you don't, I might not hit you again."

She laughed and handed over the arrows, then unslung the bow and gave that to him as well.

"Two are missing," he said, eyeing the three remaining arrows.

"Not by my hand," she said. "Okay, one was, but that was the price. What it took."

He seemed to be mad, but after a moment he took a deep breath, smiled, and said, "At this time of day I imagine our good warlord will be entertaining a cohort of other warlords at his manor. We can go over there, and when they are done I'll introduce you. But I'm telling you, if you embarrass me—"

"And my friend?" she interrupted, glancing around for Robin.

"Up here," Robin replied, working her way down one of the nearby walls. "Wanted to keep an eye out, be sure you weren't followed."

"Smart thinking."

"This way," Korak said, gesturing.

As they walked toward the large mansions on the other side of the slums, Korak kept glancing at them until Valerie finally asked him what was on his mind.

"We've heard of your type," he admitted. "Rather, the warlords have. Been discussing it, actually. There's one main guy, and you folks have got him worried."

"Us?" Robin asked.

"The Etheric Federation," he replied. "We have friends in far places, and it's not like the rest of the universe doesn't talk. We heard about the reach of the Empire first, which is now the Federation. Well, we Skulla won't be taken over so easily."

"The Federation isn't here to take anyone over," Valerie replied. "And we don't exactly represent them, anyway."

"You're human, no? And you're with the Federation?"

"Yes, and...I guess so?" Valerie shared a look with Robin, who shrugged. "I mean, yes, we are, but it's all fairly new to us. We just want to protect Earth. For us it's not about the politics, or whatever federations do, it's about making sure anyone in space with nefarious goals is stopped. Making sure we have friends in space, if you know what I mean."

Korak considered this, then smiled. "And you think the warlords will be your friends? The Bandian?"

"You don't think so, clearly."

Korak tilted his head, then tilted it back the other way as if debating what to say. "Here's the thing... *No*."

"No?"

"Not a chance. Stick around here long enough, you'll

see. You might even start to hear stories from some of the Skulla, rumors of him being on the outs."

"Only rumors, though?" Robin asked.

Again he tilted his head back and forth. "Most likely they don't have the power. You want to take down a warlord, especially *the* warlord, you need guns. You need lives to spare. You need spaceships, even. The most they can do is get themselves killed, maybe piss him off enough to get their family and friends killed too."

"Damn," Valerie interjected. "Let's hope they don't try anything stupid, then. You're not with them, I take it?"

"I am practical. If they had a chance of winning, you bet your ass I'd be in there. The Bandian might seem like the best from the outside, but many of us know better."

Soon they reached the outskirts of the slums and worked their way up a hill, where the landscape changed drastically. Instead of the desert sands of the rest of this place, up here there were lush gardens with hanging vines, flowers larger than Valerie thought were possible in colors more vibrant than she had ever seen, and strange bird-like creatures with heads that resembled those of insects.

All this surrounded the large houses, and Korak explained that much of the planet had been covered in similar vegetation at one point. Some places still were, but the pollutants of big city life had caused the vegetation to die, and when it left so did everything but the sands.

When they reached a gate of gnarled metal adorned with sculptures of fighters and more out of similar metal, Korak smiled mischievously and said, "This is the place."

**Transport Vessel En Route to SEDE**

Kalan woke to the sound of the pilot's tinny voice crackling through the speaker next to his ear.

"Heads up, boys. We're docking in five."

Kalan rubbed his eyes, trying to remember where he was and what was happening. For a moment he thought he was back in prison, but he remembered he'd been out of SEDE for five years. *Then* he remembered he was headed back.

He let out a weary sigh and stretched.

Across from him sat Bob, wide-eyed and his forehead beaded with sweat. "I can't believe you slept through the whole flight. Especially the pilot's terrible singing."

"I heard that!" the pilot barked. "I'll have you know Karli Rafittian is the greatest singer in the galaxy, and I'll proudly sing her songs. I won't be shamed."

"Yeah, you and every thirteen-year-old girl in the system," Kalan muttered. He'd never had trouble sleeping, whether he was in a quiet room or in the cargo hold of a transport ship. He figured it was a product of having spent his formative years trying to sleep in the noisy confines of Cellblock Eighteen.

He looked at Bob. "So you didn't get any sleep?"

Bob shook his head tersely. "Between his singing and your snoring, there was no way."

"Any idea how long we've been travelling?"

The man glanced down at the strange metal and glass device strapped to his wrist. "About seven hours."

"Seven hours and fourteen minutes, to be exact," the pilot interjected. "Four minutes to go."

Kalan did his best to work the blood into his limbs while still strapped into his seat. He needed to be limber in case things went bad quickly, but he wasn't going to risk unlatching his safety harness. He knew from experience that landings on SEDE could be rough.

A moment later the pilot addressed them again. "The second we land, I want your asses up here in the cockpit. I've got a few Shimmers on the payroll who'll help me unload the contraband, but if they see you they might rethink our arrangement, know what I'm saying?"

"Indeed I do," Kalan replied.

Bob's forehead was dripping now. The poor guy was getting more anxious by the minute. "So what's the plan when we get aboard?"

Kalan shifted in his seat. Strangely, he hadn't given that much thought. It had been five years since he'd been here, and he had no idea how much things had changed. Once they made their way to the cellblocks he was confident he could get to the isolation block, but he'd have to pass through a lot of guard areas to do that. His best bet at this point was to play it by ear.

"The plan is for me to find us the best route to get us there quickly and silently," Kalan explained. "That 'quickly and silently' part is essential. If we dawdle or make a racket, the Shimmers will rip our arms off our bodies before we know they're there."

"I understand."

"Do you really? Because the 'ripping the arms off' thing isn't hyperbole. I've seen them do it." He softened his tone when he saw the fear in Bob's eyes, but just a little. "Look, I'm going to do everything I can to get us through this safely, but you *have* to follow my lead. Understand?"

Bob nodded.

The whine of the engine changed to a low rumble, and Kalan was jarred in his seat as the transport touched down and attached to SEDE.

The Grayhewn had his safety harness unfastened before the pilot shouted at them through the speaker.

"Welcome to the Swarthian Extended Detention Environment, or as those of us who work here call it, 'the galaxy's armpit.' Now get up here so I can let the damn Shimmers aboard."

Kalan stood up, and waited for Bob to do the same. He noticed that the tech already had his hand on the pistol hanging from his belt.

"Bob, keep that weapon holstered unless I say otherwise. Got it?"

The man grimaced. "Who put you in charge of this mission anyway? I thought we were a team."

Kalan grabbed him by the arm and spoke in a low,

menacing tone. "On Tol or shooting through the void, maybe we're a team. Here on SEDE, I'm in charge. You do what I say, when I say. It's the only way we'll make it through this. Understand?"

Bob paused a minute, then nodded. "Yeah, fine, you're in charge."

"What's the hold-up?" the pilot snapped.

Kalan gave Bob one more hard look, then let go of his arm and headed for the cockpit.

The transport's cockpit had seating for four. The pilot gestured toward a monitor that showed the cargo hold. "I'm going to go back and get things going with the Shimmers. You two have a seat and keep your mouths shut. Shimmers can hear through concrete walls."

"You're telling me," Kalan muttered. Just about every prisoner in SEDE had been busted at some point for saying something they shouldn't have when they thought the guards weren't around, though whether that was because the guards were nearby and no one could see them or because of their excellent hearing, no one really knew. It all added to the mysterious menace of the Shimmers.

Kalan and Bob sat down and fixed their eyes on the monitor, watching as the pilot entered the cargo hold, marched to the airlock, and opened it. A moment later he stepped aside.

His voice came through speakers around them when he spoke. "Pretty much everything goes, gentlemen. If it ain't bolted down, it's meant for SEDE."

It was odd watching him speak to what appeared to be an empty cargo hold, but a moment later the crates began to move as if by their own accord. Crates that would have taken three strong men to carry lifted a foot off the ground and zipped through the airlock at an incredible rate.

"Holy hell," Bob muttered softly.

Kalan put a figure to his lips and glared at the other man. Bob got the message, and they both watched in silence as the cargo hold rapidly emptied.

The pilot stood off to the side, nearly pressing himself against the bulkhead in his effort to stay out of the way.

The whole operation took less than ten minutes. When all the crates and the boxes were gone, the pilot spoke again. "I appreciate it, boys. As always, I'll transfer your cut. Shutting the airlock."

He moved toward the airlock, but didn't close it. He turned and hurried back to the cockpit instead. "Okay, we should be clear."

Kalan considered that a moment. "How do we know they aren't still hanging out in the cargo hold?"

"I guess we don't, for sure," the pilot replied, "but they wouldn't want to get stuck in here with me, so I think it's a safe bet."

Bob's face scrunched in confusion. He started to speak, then stopped himself.

"Now how are we supposed to get past the guards to the cellblocks," Kalan mused, half to himself.

The pilot scowled. "Does that look like my problem? Duol paid me a good price to haul your asses out here, and that was exactly what I did. What you do on the other side of that airlock is no business of mine."

Kalan sighed. "Your people skills are really something. It's a wonder you ended up piloting a lonely prison transport."

Not that Kalan had much room to talk. At least this guy had a steady job.

"Thanks for the ride," he added, then slapped Bob on the arm. "Let's go."

The pilot crossed his arms and watched them leave.

When they reached the airlock, Bob held up a hand. "Hold on a second."

There was something very un-Bob-like about his serious tone, so Kalan didn't question it. He waited silently for the man to speak again.

The beady-eyed tech stuck his head through the hatch and paused a moment, then said, "Okay, let's go."

Kalan raised an eyebrow, but his instincts said to trust Bob this time. He followed Bob out of the airlock into a long metal passageway.

Everything about the place, from the antiseptic smell to the odd shade of gray everything was painted, caused eighteen years' worth of memories to come crashing back for Kalan. As far as he knew he'd never set foot in this specific passageway, but he'd been in hundreds just like it.

The last five years slipped away, and it felt like he'd never left this place.

"We're clear," Bob said softly.

"What do you mean we're—"

"Save it until we get over there," Bob said gesturing toward an area where the passage widened thirty feet ahead.

Kalan reluctantly nodded, then led the way to the spot Bob had indicated. He moved slowly and carefully, since the Shimmers could be anywhere. The axiom he'd lived by as a kid flashed like a neon sign in his brain: behave like a guard's watching over your shoulder, because he might be.

When they reached the spot, Bob stopped and turned to Kalan. "Okay, listen. I wanted to wait until we were away from the ship. If that pilot knew what I'm about to tell you, he might have decided to sell us out."

Every fiber in Kalan's being told him to keep moving, to get out of this area as quickly as possible, but Bob's words gave him pause. "Tell me."

Bob looked to the left and then to the right before saying in a low voice, "It's the Shimmers. You couldn't hear what they were saying in the cargo hold?"

"What? No, of course not. We don't even know if they have a language. If they speak, it's not on any frequency we can hear."

Bob smiled slyly. "Maybe you can't, but I can. I heard every word they said."

## 15

## Planet Tol: The Upper Manors

"Let me get this straight," Warlord Palnik said to Valerie as he paced across the wide dining room of his mansion. He lingered by an ornate chair at the head of the table like a king at his throne, and laughed. "I just need to process it. You, a human, show up and want to fight in the most dangerous, most deadly combat arena in the known universe?"

"I'm in exile," she said, passing him the cover story that she and Robin had been over and over. "My friend and I were forced out of the Etheric Federation, and now we seek a new place to live. I understand that surviving the first round of the fights gets you citizenship, and the second round grants a place to live and food stipends. So here I am."

He shook his head, not buying it for a moment, but humoring her. "Why? What could you possibly have done to get kicked out?"

"You mean because I'm an attractive female I'm harmless?"

He tilted his head from side to side, much as Korak had done. She assumed this was like shrugging.

"I assure you I'll hold my own." She glanced around, assessing the modified Skulla guards in the room to see whether any would be a real threat if she had to prove herself.

"She took a punch from me and kept fighting," Korak chimed in. He stood by the tall arched rear wall, which had the likeness of Palnik on it, made from metallic squares and triangles.

"Is that so?" Palnik stood, motioning for her to follow. "You can take a punch, but can you fight?"

"I trained for years. I've won my fair share of fights, killed my fair share of enemies."

He nodded, then held out a hand. After a moment she put hers in it and he practically choked, stepping back in disgust. "No, the ID. You have it, I assume?"

"Ah, sorry." She pulled out the chip and presented it to him.

He slid it into a slot on the table, scrutinizing the screen on the wall, and nodded. "It'll pass, but you're asking me to put myself out there. Why would I?"

"I—"

He held up a hand. "It was a rhetorical question, since I know why I would. It's because you're going to help me out."

"I am?"

"You are." He gestured to the hall, then led to them to a point where the tall archways stopped. He went through a door into a back room and she started to worry, even though he had pulled away from her hand. She would hate to have to kill him before getting his help to enter the Damu Michezo.

But instead, he led them across the dark room and stopped at a floor-to-ceiling window. He stood there with his hands behind his back, staring at three especially large houses before him.

"The Trilords," he said in awe. "The ultimate power houses. In the center you have the great Warlord Nibor, the Bandian himself. To the right, my uncle, and to the left, my greatest enemy." He turned to Valerie and said, "The one on the left, please."

"Please…what?"

"I would like you to kill the owner of the one on the left and make it look like I did it, so I can take his power. His home. *Everything*. This is my price."

"You want me to kill one of the three people in power on this planet?"

He tilted his head back and forth. "I want you to put me in that place. You want to fight and you want a friend, one who has power and information, I'm guessing. For example, I know where your ship is and I have reason to believe you're not here because of exile at all."

Valerie glared, though she had to consider that anyone on the transport ship could have overheard something and reported it to him. It wasn't unlikely.

"Tell me more about this guy." She wasn't sure if she was stalling or really considering this, but figured knowing more about the situation couldn't hurt. "Why is he your enemy?"

"How about I tell you what makes him worth killing instead?"

Palnik leaned in, eyes narrowed. "That manoa licker has had more slaves publicly executed—for entertainment, mind you—than any other warlord. He rose to power purely by forcing others to fight, then taking percentages of their earnings and stakes in their holdings. He's risen to power on the backs of those beneath him, often breaking those backs along the way."

"While you and the other warlords haven't?"

"Let's just say we're disgusted by what he's done and leave it at that."

"I don't run around killing for the fun of it," she replied, "or because someone asks me too."

He tilted his head. "This isn't for either of those reasons. This is to bring justice to a murderer, it's to get you into that fight, so that you might fulfill your mission."

She considered that, wondering if her translator had accurately translated the word "justice." That was a soft spot for her, but he couldn't have any way of knowing that. She sighed, knowing she didn't really have any other options here. "And when they try to find the killer?"

"When he dies his power goes to the victor, as long as the killer is in the same class. Anyone lower would be publicly executed, naturally."

"You have a messed-up system here," Valerie observed dryly. "From what I've gathered, people live in absolute poverty unless they earn their spots among the citizens by fighting. Fights, I might add, that result in death more times than not. At a certain point they can earn their way into the upper crust, where you all plot to kill each other. If successful, you take everything from the dead with no consequences. Is that about right?"

He nodded. "Messed-up, though? Hardly. It encourages us to be strong, which is why the others in our system and those surrounding us know we're not to be challenged."

"Uh huh." All she could think was how helping him would just put one more lunatic in a higher position of power. Then again, she would have what she needed. Perhaps there would be another way around it, but she had a feeling all the warlords would have similar requests. At least this one presented himself as friendly enough.

"When you're done with your moral judgments, let me know what you've decided."

"You have a deal." There was no reason to think about it. Accept, make sure the other guy was evil, and do it. If she found any reason *not* to kill him, that was the way it would be. She'd start looking at other options then, but for now there was no reason to make him think she would be anything other than compliant.

"Very well." He motioned to the houses again. "You have your mission. When it's over, you'll get your reward."

She spent the next couple hours lingering in the shadows of the target's house, learning that Skulla didn't sleep normal hours. At least these didn't—the sun had been down for some time and yet the Skulla still meandered about, some cooking, others returning from what appeared to be gambling, stealing, and worse, if their brags could be believed.

Finally she noticed a floating dome approaching—like a palanquin, she supposed. Judging by the surrounding guards it had to be her target, Warlord Charbon.

Working her way up the side of the mansion, she used a sculpture for leverage to push herself to the ledge above. Each step could lead to her falling here, but her senses were alert and she moved with skill. Soon she was at the balcony, but the door was locked.

Using her vampire strength, she pushed the hand-recognition plate and was in.

Now she moved as fast as she could. Faster than seemed necessary, but she wanted to be in place and ready. Was he as big a scumbag as Palnik had made him out to be? As dastardly as his followers?

Guards roamed the halls, some at windows and some elsewhere. At first she moved through the shadows with such speed that none saw her, but the door to what she guessed to be the master bedroom was guarded by several guards. She could take them out, or go back outside and try the window.

After a moment's consideration she realized the window would likely be guarded anyway, so she might as well deal with these and be done with it.

She descended on them like the vampires of old, sliding along the wall using her claws and pouncing with exposed fangs when they looked up. It must have been a terrifying sight, she thought, as she landed on them and went to work, tossing one after another over the side of the stairs. They shouted as they fell and thumped at the bottom, but were not loud enough to raise any alarms. They were likely all in shock.

Her feet hit the ground softly when she followed them and ended their lives. Leaving them unconscious would've possibly worked, but then they would've been able to identify her and likely cause trouble with the fighting contest.

For the Etheric Federation's and Earth's safety, she couldn't risk it.

Besides, these were the closest followers of a very bad man. If nothing else, they were guilty by association.

This suspicion was proven true when he finally appeared, large doors sliding open and a strange glow filling the room.

"Where have those guards gotten to?" Warlord Charbon asked, then strolled up the steps, cursing along the way. "Off whoring again, no doubt. We'll see if they're better guards when I have them gelded. See how they like that."

Valerie could see his outline from her hiding spot, and when the light hit the edge of his Skulla robes she noticed dark stains. Blood?

A scream came from the other room, and Charbon paused at his door. "Tell them to shut their mouths. Bring them here so I can finish this."

Valerie didn't wait to see what was coming, but instead surged up the steps and grabbed this male by the throat—loosely enough that he could talk, but tightly enough to let him know she could take his life at any second.

"Who are they?" she asked.

He glared, confused.

"You have a translator chip, right?" she asked.

After another moment he nodded. "I understand, and I hope you understand that you'll be dead in a matter of minutes. When my guards—"

His voice caught as she held him out over the edge of the stairs so he could see their bodies at the bottom.

"Your guards are gone," she said. "You'll join them soon enough, but first... What were the screams?"

"People who didn't pay. As is my right, their lives are forfeit."

"As in 'taxes?'"

"Close enough," he replied.

"You get to torture—I'm assuming from the blood and screams—and then kill them...because they didn't pay you some sort of tax?" She shook her head, remembering the people she had kicked out of New York for less than that. The former leader she had hunted down and killed, because he had instituted a fear-based tyranny much like this seemed to be.

"And you?" he asked. "Who made you judge, so that you can come here and kill my men? Is that any more just?"

She frowned, then twisted her hand and squeezed to crush his larynx. When his body hit the floor she finished him off with a stomp to the head, so hard that it crushed his skull like an overripe watermelon.

It wasn't about those types of questions anymore. She was a soldier, part of the greater system, here to fulfill that purpose. As far as she could tell this male would be a hindrance to that system; her enemy in any sense of the word. At least, it was clear he soon would have been.

Dragging him back to his room, she gave the signal. Robin would bring Palnik so that he could take credit for this and stroll out a victor, the wielder of more than twice as much power as he'd had before.

And if he didn't deliver on his promise? Well, then there'd be one more warlord losing his life tonight.

## Swarthian Extended Detention Environment (SEDE)

Kalan stared at Bob in disbelief. "What do you *mean* you can hear the Shimmers? *Nobody* can hear the Shimmers."

Bob shrugged. "I can. Plain as I hear you right now."

"How the hell is that possible?"

Bob considered that for a moment before answering. "I assume you've got some kind of translation chip, right?"

"Of course. They implant them when we're born. Pretty much everybody in the Vurugu system has one, aside from a few remote cultures who don't interact with others."

The translation chips were more than a convenience to avoid having to learn the languages of other species—they were an absolute necessity. The Skulla's mouths were unique in that they had two tongues—a smaller one that nestled underneath the first. Because of this, it was physically impossible for other species to recreate the sounds that made up their language.

"Okay, well, I've got one too," Bob said. "The way I figure it, I have a better model. Nothing but the best for the universe's elite."

"Huh." Kalan wondered if it could really be that simple.

On the other hand, he'd had his chip implanted here on SEDE. It made sense that they wouldn't want the prisoners to be able to hear the guards. They used an artificial voice through the PA system when they needed to convey something important, and it gave the Shimmers the advantage of being able to talk freely without the prisoners' even knowing they were there.

"What did they say in the cargo hold?" Kalan asked.

"Nothing very interesting. They really dislike our pilot, and they talked about the ways they'd dismember him if not for the profits they made off his operation. They're a creative bunch, I'll give them that. They chattered nonstop from the moment they boarded. Point is, I'll listen for them coming as we move through the ship. That should help, right?"

"Hell yeah, it will."

"So what's the plan?"

Kalan scratched at an old scar on his shoulder while he thought. He'd promised Bob they'd figure things out when they boarded SEDE, and now here they were. It was time to stop thinking and start doing.

He gestured down the hall ahead of them. "I think our best bet is to get to the observation deck. They herd a whole mess of prisoners there throughout the day, and if we can reach it we should be able to get lost in the general population. Then when they call them back to their cells, we can slip into the cellblock with them."

Bob raised an eyebrow. "They won't notice two random weirdos who shouldn't be there? One a huge Grayhewn and the other a highly attractive human?"

"Human, huh?" Kalan realized he'd never thought to ask the name of Valerie's and her friends' species. "Okay, look… You've got to remember that SEDE is first and foremost a spaceship. It doesn't run like a normal prison, it's more like a flying city where the guards regularly come and mess with the residents. The prisoners have to scan in every hour or the guards descend on them like it's meal-time in the yanecat pen, but I seriously doubt they're on the lookout for *extra* prisoners."

Bob nodded. "I guess that makes sense. Prisons are designed to keep people in, not out."

"Exactly." Kalan glanced nervously down the corridor. "I guess we'd better get moving."

They spent the next hour slowly and meticulously making their way through the massive ship. Almost as much time was spent stopped while Bob listened for the Shimmers as moving toward their objective.

Kalan quickly oriented himself to where they were on the ship, and he led them on a roundabout route via small rarely-used corridors.

When they were almost to their destination they had their first bout of bad luck. They were in an especially narrow corridor approaching a blind left turn when Bob froze in his tracks and the color drained from his face.

"Kalan," he said, his voice little more than a whisper. "Someone's coming around the corner."

The Grayhewn cursed silently. He'd heard nothing, but then he wouldn't, would he?

He leaned close to Bob's ear. "Okay, we'll spread out and stretch our arms wide. When he rounds that corner he'll run into one of us, and then we grab him and don't let go until he's dead."

Bob hesitated, then nodded.

They did as Kalan had instructed, each spreading his arms as far as he could. Kalan was relieved that they were able to span the width of the passage. There was no way anyone would get past them.

He didn't dare speak, but he could see from the tension on Bob's face that the guard was almost upon them. He tensed himself, waiting.

Something came around the corner and slammed into his chest. He rocked backward, almost losing his balance, but he threw an arm around the creature and held on tightly. His other hand went to his weapon.

Kalan had no idea what part of the creature he had grabbed. It felt sharp and boney—a shoulder perhaps? It struck him that he had no idea what Shimmer anatomy was like. For all he knew they didn't *have* shoulders.

Shoulder or not, he jammed the barrel of his Tralen-14 into the creature's body and pulled the trigger.

The creature was flailing madly now, but Kalan held fast. He ran his gun up the creature's body, trying to find the head. He pressed the barrel against the hard knob at about his shoulder height and, hoping he had guessed correctly, fired again.

After a moment the creature went slack in his arms.

"I think he's dead," Bob announced. "At least, he's not screaming anymore. He called you a son of a prison trench... I guess that's an insult?"

Kalan lowered the invisible creature to the ground. He was still shocked at the knowledge that the Shimmer had only come up to his shoulder. In his mind they'd always been massive creatures who towered over him.

"Any idea if he got off a signal to his buddies?"

Bob shook his head. "I don't think so, since he was cursing you the whole time. Though the way he was screaming his head off, I wouldn't be surprised if someone heard."

Kalan grimaced, but there was nothing they could do about that now. If the guards were going to descend on them, so be it. "We'd better keep moving."

They proceeded more quickly and much less cautiously than they had at first, their primary goal being to get far away from the fallen guard as quickly as possible. Even if no other Shimmers had heard their dying friend's screams, someone was bound to stumble across the body sooner or later and they needed to be out of sight when that happened.

Kalan led them to a place where a narrow corridor joined a larger one. "We'll wait here," he said softly.

It was a risk. The wider corridor was heavily trafficked so the chance of a Shimmer wandering by were much greater, but if they wanted to get to the observation deck, then this was the place to be.

He leaned toward Bob and whispered, "They lead a new set of prisoners through here every hour for their time on the observation deck. When that happens, we'll fall in with the group."

As they waited, Kalan did his best not to think too hard about what was about to happen. Even if everything went exactly as planned, he was going to return to the blocks. Best case scenario, that meant there would be at least three gangs out to kill him. He'd burned more than a few bridges in his final months on SEDE.

He wasn't sure how long they waited. It could have been ten minutes or thirty, but eventually they heard the unmistakable sound of prisoners approaching.

Bob's eyes widened as he realized how many prisoners were coming down the corridor.

"That's just a tenth of the total," Kalan said, noticing the look on Bob's face. "Now do you understand why I think it's going to be easy to sneak in among them?" Kalan paused. "We'll wait until a couple hundred have passed, then we'll slip into the crowd.

They silently pressed against the wall of the narrow corridor, hoping none of the passersby could see them. The approaching mass of prisoners brought something back that Kalan hadn't thought about in a long time: the noise of SEDE. He'd spent his first eighteen years in a constant cacophony. Prison was a lot of things, but quiet had never been one of them.

Kalan watched the prisoners as they hurried past, wondering how many of them would ever get out of SEDE and whether they'd be able to make something of their lives when they did. Or would they be sold into the fighting pits on Tol?

A face in the crowd caught Kalan's attention, and the breath halted in his throat.

He grabbed Bob's arm. "Come on, we're going."

"I thought we were waiting until—"

Kalan didn't wait for him to finish, but stepped into the throng and pulled Bob along with him.

He edged between the prisoners, ignoring their annoyed shouts, and made his way toward the face he'd spotted.

It wasn't long before he reached his target. He hesitated only a moment, then touched her shoulder. She turned, and her eyes widened when she saw him.

Kalan forced the lump in his throat down and flashed her a smile. "Hi, Mom."

## 16

## Planet Tol: The House of Charbon

Valerie glanced at the dead, broken form of Charbon one last time before walking from the room. Her gut churned with a strange mixture of emotions—guilt, mixed with the thrill of success. This wasn't her planet, but she was pulling strings here like their lives revolved around her mission for the Etheric Federation.

It was almost laughable how guilty she felt about taking out this Charbon bastard. He was a warlord. A murderer. A piece of shit by any definition. And after all, it had needed to be done.

She stopped in the foyer at the sight of Warlord Palnik and pulled herself together, standing up straight. If she was going to make this happen, fulfill her duty here, she couldn't waste time questioning her actions after they were already done. She had a duty to her people. To Earth.

"It's done, then?" Palnik asked in his wheezing voice.

She nodded.

"A promise is a promise." Palnik turned to one of the women at his side. "See that our friend here is properly entered into the Damu Michezo on behalf of Warlord Palnik. She will be tested at sundown."

"Tested?" Valerie asked.

He cocked his head and sneered. "Surely you understand at least some of our culture?" When she didn't answer, he shook his head and added, "Just be in my courtyard tonight, where the selection committee will confirm your entrance. I'm sure it will be no problem at all for the likes of you. We have the letter of introduction, you've done your part here, and all that remains is the trial."

She wasn't sure what that meant, but nodded her appreciation. "I'll be there."

"Will you join us in the ceremony room for my ascension?" he asked with an excited sparkle in his eyes. "It's one of our traditions that's not to be missed."

"We'll be along shortly," Valerie replied, watching as his men dragged off the body of his late competitor.

It wasn't until he was out of earshot that Robin let out an annoyed sigh and said, "I don't know. It doesn't feel right."

"As if this did?"

"I mean, no…" Robin grimaced. "But that guy—"

"Is our only hope of making it into the fight right now," Valerie interrupted. "Once that's over, anything goes."

Robin nodded, and the two made their way to what was formerly Warlord Charbon's great hall, but was now, according to local tradition, Warlord Palnik's, along with the former warlord's surviving fighters, slaves, and family.

They were arrayed in a militaristic formation, these

attendees, with the recently deceased Warlord's family on their knees at the front. While the servants and slaves were dressed in loose clothing of white and yellow, the family members and their soldiers wore as little clothing as possible to better show off their tattoos. It was a pride thing, Valerie guessed, maybe even associated with rank in this society. Dresses hung loosely from the women's shoulders and left their backs and sides completely bare, while the men were adorned in skirts that glimmered like metal, along with shoulder bracers with green lights along the edges.

It was a strange style, one she had yet to see here. Then again, she hadn't been to an ascension ceremony, either.

Warlord Palnik stepped forward as his guards threw the corpse at his feet not more than three paces from the family. Gasps sounded, and a choked sob.

"You all belong to me now," Palnik said, and with a swift movement he had pulled forth a blade that glowed red at a press of a button. He cut through the neck, separating Charbon's head from his body in a quick motion that cauterized the flesh behind it. The aftereffect was a horrible stench, but no mess. Holding the head high, Palnik kept his eyes on the family. "By the governing body of Tol as recognized by all leadership in the Vurugu system, any defiance will be met with death. You are all mine by right, as are your slaves and other property."

There was a long silence, during which Valerie tasted bile and had to fight down an urge to slap the skin right off Palnik's face. A glance at Robin showed red cheeks and wild eyes, and she knew the younger woman was struggling twice as hard to keep herself together.

Back on Earth, when the vampires had taken Robin from her family, they had turned her but enslaved her parents up north. The two women had rescued them eventually, but not until after many sleepless nights of wondering what had become of them.

"It won't stand," Valerie whispered to her friend.

"What won't?" Robin asked, also in a whisper.

"This." Valerie bit her lip to keep her voice from rising. "Their system. Slavery, fighting to the death—all of it. When they're with the Etheric Federation, it won't last."

"And you have all the answers in that regard?" Robin folded her arms tightly across her chest. "We can't take down a whole planet by ourselves, and we both know that wouldn't be within our mandate anyway."

"You'd have a problem with that?"

"Hell, no." Robin pursed her lips, eyes narrowed. "You know I'm with you, Val. Anything you say—as long as it's not ass-backwards craziness—you can count on me. But I know that we're part of something bigger out here, and feel I should be the voice of reason when necessary."

Valerie had to really work to not raise her voice as she hissed, "You're saying I don't make sense?" Instead of waiting for a response, she added, "Listen, if it comes to it we'll get ahold of TH. Clear it with the Federation first. All right?"

Robin nodded, then glanced behind them. "What do you say we get out of here? They saw us, so they know we attended."

As far as Valerie was concerned they never should have come, and now she couldn't leave fast enough.

They made their way through the intricate halls of this

building, so much the opposite of what they had seen in the areas where most of the people of Tol lived. Intense metal carvings, focused on jagged edges and pyramid shapes, lined the walls. Lights hung from the ceilings, glowing in a way that better represented natural light, something lights back on Earth had never gotten quite right.

Neither spoke until they were outside and moving through the gardens, which contained tall spires and angular sculptures again, interspersed with flowers that resembled dragons' mouths and lions with their manes.

"How can such a horrible place be so beautiful?" Robin asked.

"It was disgusting," Valerie agreed, nodding.

"Not so unlike our older civilizations, though," Robin stated.

"Excuse me?"

"I read a thing or two." She shrugged. "I mean, when I found those old books in Toronto, I insisted my parents bring them to New York. What do you think I did all that time?"

"Train to fight, like me?"

Robin laughed, though it was less about mirth and more to do with what seemed right at the moment. "No, I was reading. The...ancient Serbians, I think it was? Stories about how they would do terrible things to their enemies after capturing them. When the Persians defeated them, in many ways they were viewed as liberators coming in to stop those horrific acts. Many others saw them in a similar way, but they didn't know how that worked relative to what had come before."

"You're saying we're not so different from these people?"

She shrugged. "I saw enough on Earth to not argue with that statement, but no. What I was saying was that we'd be like the Persians. We might have to do some bad things to take out the current leadership, make a change here, but it's all relative."

"Sure." Valerie nodded, glancing back to ensure nobody was watching or listening. "You can bet we won't be sawing off people's heads in front of their families."

They made their way out of the city to the spot where they had left the *Grandeur,* and were glad to find that Garcia and Flynn had taken care of themselves as far as food was concerned.

They had even found some ground meat snacks wrapped in pink leaves, which Valerie thought she might try later.

"Are you in?" Flynn asked.

"In like Flynn," Valerie replied, then held up a hand. "I know, I know. Making stupid jokes to compensate for having to watch a man's head being removed from his body."

Garcia shook his head. "It's the same everywhere, isn't it? Fight the crazies back home, fight the crazies out here. It never stops."

"Except that," Robin glanced at the ceiling of the ship as though looking at all of space, "out here there're about a quajillion more beings, and therefore a much greater likelihood of there being even more crazies."

"Ever wonder if it's actually we who are the crazy ones?" Flynn asked. "I mean, who the fuck goes to some alien planet and *tries* to get themselves thrown into a death competition?"

"I can't tell if you're being a dick, or…" Valerie eyed him, then chuckled, and he laughed. "That's what I thought. Are we crazy? Damn straight! But crazy in a good way, not crazy in a 'I'm gonna piss in your skull' way."

"Ick! If we meet any of those, please let me know so I can run the other way."

"Will do," she agreed.

"So what's the plan, then?" Garcia asked. "From here, what's the strategy?"

"Learn what you can without drawing too much attention to yourselves," Valerie replied. "Has anyone given you a hard time so far?"

Garcia shook his head.

"It's like they're so used to weird aliens showing up," Flynn chimed in, "that we're just one more oddity. Since everyone's strange, strange is normal."

"Good. Keep your ears open, and I don't just mean about the fight system. I mean about society. I've been hearing things, observing the way the lower classes look at the elites. Something's up."

"And us?" Robin asked, her eyelids heavy.

"You look about as beat as I feel," Valerie replied honestly. "We might not need as much sleep as we used to, but we still need to rest occasionally. Get some sleep if you can, or simply close your eyes if not. The body needs it."

"Roger that," Robin said, with the first genuine smile that day. "Roger-the-fuck that."

She staggered off to follow her orders.

"You two managed to rest, I take it?" Valerie asked the other two.

"We got back early, had a romantic picnic, and slept together," Garcia said with a wink to Flynn.

"That's not... He didn't mean that." Flynn flushed. "Listen, I would never—"

"You got something against Garcia here, or the idea of stuff like that in general?" Valerie raised her eyebrows, waiting.

"I-I don't think it'd be smart of me to answer that," Flynn replied.

"Clever man," she replied. "All right, as long as you two rested, I don't care if you spooned or—"

"Ack, we didn't!" Flynn stood tall, the vein in his neck bulging.

Both Garcia and Valerie burst into laughter.

"Listen, buddy," Garcia said. "She knows I'm joking. Lighten up."

Flynn frowned, then leaned back and attempted to put on his best smile. "Yeah, I knew that. Me too."

"Sure you did."

"You two take watch, then," Valerie said, heading out to get some rest too. "Anything fishy, wake me."

She found her bunk and curled up on her side, glancing at Robin to see if she had already passed out. Probably happened as soon as her head hit the pillow. The woman's lower lip stuck out in a cute way when she slept, and Valerie felt she could lie there for hours staring at it.

But that wasn't hers to do, not anymore. Here it was about being professional, not letting silly things like emotions get in the way of her duty. Maybe someday, when this war was over and Earth was safe... Maybe then she could explore that path again.

Still, those thoughts couldn't keep out the memories that flooded into her mind as she drifted off to sleep. That day on the airship at Slaver's Peak when they had freed a group of slaves and were off to Toro to rescue Robin's parents...that was the last time they had been romantic. The last time she remembered feeling those soft lips against hers, Robin's warm breath in her ear when the woman had moved to kiss her neck but paused to shudder with anticipation.

It was with those thoughts of a time with a different Robin—the same physical woman, and yet everything between them changed—that Valerie found herself drifting off to sleep.

## 17

**Swarthian Extended Detention Environment (SEDE)**

Kalan woke up early, strangely refreshed after a night in his childhood cot. He tried to push away thoughts of the things he needed to do that day. Break into the most secure wing of the prison, get a political prisoner out, find a way off this ship… It was best not to think about that. Not yet.

For now, Kalan wanted to enjoy being in his childhood apartment and seeing his mother.

He sat up to find Bob upright in the cot across from him, clearly not sharing his hopeful tranquility. There were dark circles under his eyes and he looked positively pissed.

"Morning," Kalan said. "How'd you sleep?"

Bob scowled. "Between your snoring, the constant shouts and screams coming from the other cells, and this rock-hard cot? Not great. Not great at all."

Kalan raised his arms and stretched, his shoulders cracking as he worked the stiffness from them. "We prefer to call them apartments, not cells."

"Whatever!" Bob said. "All I know is, I'm glad I only have to spend one night here."

"Assuming we don't get caught," Kalan pointed out.

He stood up and walked to the sink, and splashed a little water on his face. The previous evening had been a whirlwind reunion with his mother. Her reaction upon seeing him had been a strange combination of shock, delight, and horror. Her understandable first assumption had been that he had been arrested and convicted, but once he'd alleviated that fear she had been much more excited to see him.

She'd still given him a hell of a time for being stupid enough to come back voluntarily.

Much to Kalan's surprise, Bob and his mother had gotten along quite well. They'd even ganged up on him a little, teasing him about his serious nature.

All these thoughts were running through Kalan's head when he heard the yelling from outside.

"Grayhewn!"

A feeling of dread crept into Kalan's stomach. He recognized that voice, and it represented a problem he did not need this morning.

"*Grayhewn!*" the familiar voice called again. "I know you're hiding behind your mama in there. Come out and face me or we'll come in after you."

Kalan patted his face with a towel and sighed. It appeared there would be no getting around this.

He turned to find Bob staring out the window with a look of horror on his face. "What the hell *is* that thing?"

Kalan's mother Gara answered from the doorway. "It's a walking, talking piece of shit named Zoras, and he controls the black market in this cellblock. Kalan was dumb enough to piss him off the day before he got out."

Bob glanced at Kalan. "What possessed you to do that?"

Kalan peered through the hole that served as a window, confirming that Zoras was just as ugly as he remembered. "He punched a friend of mine in the face. I punched back."

"He doesn't take kindly to that sort of thing," Gara explained.

Kalan looked at her again, unable to keep the smile off his face at the sight of her. She was taller than he was, but lean and muscular. She bore a few lines around her eyes, but other than that she didn't look a bit different than she had five years ago. That she'd managed to survive in this crowded, dangerous co-ed prison while so many of her fellow prisoners had not was a testament to both her brilliance and her grit.

"Well, I guess I'd better go beat him up again," Kalan said wearily.

"Have fun, dear," Gara said, a twinkle in her eye.

"Thanks, Ma." He paused beside the cot to consider the Tralen-14, but he left it where it lay. The Shimmers didn't much care if prisoners beat the shit out of each other or smuggled in contraband, but guns were where they drew the line. Using the Tralen would be a surefire way to attract their attention.

"You want me to come with you?" From the tone of Bob's voice, it was clear he was only asking to be polite.

"Nah, I got this."

Kalan stepped out of the apartment and onto what the prisoners called "the street." When SEDE was constructed, each cellblock had been intended to look like its own little town. The cells had walk-up stoops to make them resemble the luxury apartments on the Skulla planet Stais, and the walkway between the cells was concrete painted to look like cobblestone.

Over the years the place had fallen into disrepair, and the governments behind SEDE weren't about to put up the necessary funds to maintain the facade of a city. Now the cell blocks looked more like a town a hundred years after an apocalyptic event.

Zoras stood in the center of the street glaring up at Gara's home. Kalan carefully made his way down the broken stairs.

"Hello, Zoras. How've you been?"

Zoras was a modified Skulla, the product of one of the Bandian's many genetic experiments. He stood no taller than the average Skulla, but he was so muscular that he was nearly as wide as he was tall. It made him quite strange to behold.

"Grayhewn, seeing you back aboard has made my day," he said with a smile. "My week, even! I'm going to make your life a living hell. What'd they get you for?"

"Clobbering guys who yelled at my mom's house first thing in the morning."

Zoras scowled. "That's how it's going to be?"

Kalan shrugged. "I'm on a tight schedule, so if you want to get your revenge or something it's now or never. Or, we could forget the past and move on with our lives. Your call."

Zoras clearly didn't know how to respond to that. He stared blankly at Kalan for a long moment.

A Pallicon shouted through a window, "Kill him, Zoras!"

That was all the encouragement the Skulla needed. In one motion he crouched and launched himself at Kalan.

It was like a massive spring uncoiling. The Skulla flew at Kalan with such speed and force that the Grayhewn had no chance of dodging the assault. Zoras slammed into him and wrapped his arms around Kalan's body, knocking him to the ground.

The Skulla then sat on Kalan's chest, crushing him and making it difficult to breathe. Pinning Kalan's arms down with his knees, Zoras drew back his fist and punched Kalan in the temple.

It was like getting hit by a falling tree; the world swam in front of Kalan's eyes. He knew he couldn't take many more hits like that.

Thankfully, like all of the Bandian's failed genetic experiments Zoras had a weakness. His body was covered with impossibly thick muscle, but his head—that was standard-issue.

Kalan squirmed, making it appear like he was trying to free his right arm. When Zoras shifted his weight slightly to put more pressure on it, Kalan pulled hard with his left.

Just as he'd hoped, the arm popped out from under Zoras' knee.

He threw a quick jab at Zoras' nose, and then another, and a third. He continued pummeling the Skulla's head and face, throwing punches so fast that Zoras wasn't able to do much other than rock back in pain with each hit.

Finally Kalan gave a mighty heave and rolled the big Skulla off him.

Without giving him time to recover, he pounced and rained blows on him with both hands.

When Zoras stopped struggling to get out from under him Kalan knew the fight was over. He got up and brushed himself off.

"Pleasure as always." He started to walk away, but Zoras spoke.

"Kill you... Get my friends... Watch your back, Grayhewn. We'll kill you." His words were a bit garbled due to his busted lips, but Kalan had no trouble understanding the message.

"Yeah, well, you'll have to find me first." He sneered and walked back into his mother's apartment.

Gara and Bob had watched through the window. The human smiled widely and pumped his fist as Kalan entered, but Gara shook her head, a slight smile on her face.

"Sorry, Mom. I hope I didn't cause trouble for you."

Gara shrugged. "No more than I'm used to."

Bob frowned. "Wait, is that guy going to come after you?"

"Probably," the female answered. "I'm not worried, though."

"You're not?"

Kalan chuckled. "Who do you think taught me to fight?"

Gara's expression turned serious. "I think it's time for the two of you to get going. There's a chance Zoras' gang will try to retaliate. I doubt they'd make a serious move against me, but you..."

"Yeah," Kalan said with a sigh. "I suppose so, but I wish we could spend more time together." He felt a pang of sadness as he spoke. What neither of them was saying—what neither *would* say—was that in all likelihood this would be goodbye forever.

He consoled himself with the knowledge that they'd been through a long goodbye once already. They'd never expected to see each other again, so this visit was an unexpected gift.

His mother touched his arm. "There's so much I need to tell you—things I probably should have told you long ago—but things have changed now and I don't know how to—"

"You don't have to, Ma."

"I do." She slipped something into his hand. "Read this when you get out of here."

He looked at the microchip in his hand. "What's on this?"

"There's no time to explain it now. Just watch. Later." She paused for a moment as if there were more she wanted to say, but then she set her jaw.

"Thanks, Ma," Kalan said. "I, um, left something for you by the cot I slept in last night. I thought it might come in handy."

She nodded, curious but not wanting to get into a discussion on another topic. It was clear she wanted to rip off this bandage, painful as that might be. "I got up while you boys were still sleeping and talked to Etter, the Pallicon who lives at the upper end of the block. He delivers food to the isolation block."

"He thinks he can get us in?" Kalan asked.

"Sure. *In* is not a problem."

"Yeah, yeah, it's getting out that's the issue," Bob said. "I keep hearing that."

"That's because it's true. Now get going—you have work to do."

## Planet Tol: The *Singlaxian Grandeur*

When Valerie woke she glanced at Robin's bed, which was freshly made. A bite of her lip brought back the memories she had fallen to sleep to, and she felt a pang of guilt. Robin was her friend, a fellow soldier in this fight against the evil of the universe. She couldn't keep thinking of her in that other way.

Throwing her legs over the side of the bunk, she lingered for a moment to clear her thoughts and focus on the day's goal. She had found that the best way to enter a fight was with a clear head. If she could imagine herself landing a roundhouse kick, each step and movement clear in her head, then the actions would later come as instinct. At this point they *were* instinct without a doubt, but distracting thoughts could be a major hindrance.

A song blasted from the bridge and she smiled, tapping her foot to the beat and wondering what it was. She pushed herself to her feet a moment later and joined the others. Flynn and Robin there, both nodding along, Flynn laughing at something Robin had just said.

The way he was eyeing her made Valerie realize she wasn't the only one distracted here.

"Garcia?"

"Keeping watch," Flynn said. "He's making the rounds, checking for any signs of trouble. I gotta say, though…

Based on how it's been so far, it's possible we're all acting a bit paranoid."

"I'd say that since this is our first experience on an alien planet, a hostile one no less, we're being the exact right amount of paranoid."

Flynn shrugged, then smiled at Robin again. The fact that he didn't say anything made it quite awkward, though.

"I'll just…" Robin gestured to the back door where the lavatory was.

Unfortunately the upgrades hadn't removed their need for bodily functions like pissing. If Valerie could have had her way she would have also removed the romance bugs, sleepiness, and itchiness. No matter how indestructible she felt she still got a case of the scratchies sometimes, and it pissed her off.

"Yeah, I'll use it when you're done and then," she leaned down to glance out, confirming from the darkening sky and lines of orange in the clouds that it was nearly sunset, "we should head to Palnik's. I'm anxious to get this over with."

Robin nodded and went to the head, leaving Flynn and Valerie alone. Possibly for the first time ever.

Valerie realized this and cocked her head, staring at the corporal. "What's your deal, anyway?"

"In what way?"

"I asked Colonel Walton to assign you to this team because I saw what you could do in the ring. But can you do it in a real life or death situation?"

Flynn scrunched his face as if debating whether to take that as an insult, but then his smile returned. "Put me in combat and I'll show you."

"So you're hot stuff?"

"I'm not *cold* stuff. I'm sure as hell not a corpse, and won't be anytime soon."

"What?" Valerie licked her lips, trying to understand what he was talking about. "Yes or no, can you kick some alien ass into the next star system if needed?"

He wiped the smile from his face, returning her stern gaze. "You better believe it."

"But I whipped him good," Garcia said from the doorway as he stepped back into the *Grandeur*. "You all saw it, right?"

"That was sparring," Flynn argued. "Doesn't count."

"How the hell do you figure that?"

"With sparring I'm always scared to hurt the other person. You get carried away, you make enemies. I'd rather lose and not break your leg than vice-versa." His face went pale and he turned to Valerie, cringing. "Oh, sorry."

He was referring to how, much to Valerie's surprise, Colonel Walton had busted her knee in a sparring session. Other than that the trip had been quite exciting, what with finally getting to meet Bethany Anne and seeing Michael again.

She waved the comment off, lifting her leg and moving the lower portion. "Seems to be working well enough. No harm done."

"No lasting harm, anyway," Robin added as she returned from the head. "You're up."

Valerie nodded and started to walk out, but paused and glanced back. "Everyone, suit up. I want you all carrying, but concealed. We can't start any problems, but I'd rather see this whole planet burn than any of you hurt. Understood?"

"Yes, ma'am," they all replied, and went about it.

They set off, Robin walking at Valerie's side, Garcia and Flynn already veering off in another direction, so that they wouldn't all be seen entering town together. It was Valerie's idea to stay separate—so that if she got into trouble, they might still be able to operate without immediately being suspect as well.

Finding the house wasn't hard. Aside from simply retracing their steps, there weren't that many who had earned the title of warlord, it seemed. Or if there were, there weren't many of this rank, or at least many who had houses this size.

Now, thanks to Valerie, he had two of them. If the fallen warlord's army would be loyal to him, he would now have an army large enough to take down much of the others, she imagined.

"Earth was never like this, right?" Robin asked. "I mean, there were the slums for the crazy people up in Toro, before we stopped all that. But I mean, where it's just so...segregated?"

Valerie considered New York as it had been rebuilt, considering the parts of town where the drugged out looking people had lived. Those brick buildings failed in comparison with the building Sandra and Diego had taken up residence in, her old closest friends.

"Sorry to say it," Valerie replied, "but I think it was *exactly* like this. In some ways, still is."

"Kinda hurts when you put a lens to yourself," Robin

admitted. "If we ever go back, let's make sure this isn't a thing anymore."

"Not if, *when*."

They turned down a street that led them past some merchant Skulla, a group performing a very angular dance for the rest, their foreheads covered with sharp, pointed tattoos.

"I'd love to sit down with and ask them what those tattoos mean sometime," Valerie said. "They have to have meaning, right?"

"If it were me, I'd get a little unicorn on my forehead for every person I could've killed but didn't." Robin chuckled, apparently finding herself quite funny, but Valerie simply rolled her eyes in response. "Come on, unicorns are cool!"

"Dear, I'm sorry to tell you this, but considering that we can heal from a sword in a kidney, I doubt a tattoo would stay very well."

Robin thought about it for a moment, then said, "Damn, there goes my unicorn-tattoo dream. Maybe if I went really, really, *really* deep with the ink?"

"How deep can you go into your forehead?" Valerie laughed. "Shut up."

"What?" Robin tried to hide her grin. "A girl can dream. I'm surprised you even know what a unicorn is."

"I think you told me about them…maybe? Someone did. They weren't real though, right?"

Robin shrugged. "I hope they were. Honestly, they were mentioned in these pages of an old book I found half-burned. What was there sounded awesome." She paused in thought as they took another turn; the large houses were now in front of them. "T.S. Raul. I think that was the author name."

"I don't think it matters much," Valerie said, "I mean, he can't still be alive, can he?"

"Maybe, if he became a vampire."

"Touché." Valerie got lost in thought at that for a moment, wondering how many vampires were left on Earth and how many there had ever been. Was it possible some famous people she had heard about had become vampires and never really died? The fact that she didn't actually know much about famous people made the question fade really fast. All she had been familiar with were stories of old French rulers, some author who wrote a story about a teddy bear that goes into their land after monsters to save his kid, and now this T.S. Raul or whatever person.

They were passing the water reservoir, a highly guarded building of dull brown metal, when a shot rang out.

At first she couldn't process it, but then she saw Robin wobble and collapse. Blood was seeping from her right breast and the cloth was singed on her back.

"Damn, should've...worn the...body armor," Robin gasped as she clutched the wound.

"Good thing about that healing," Valerie offered.

"Fuck you, it...hurts."

Valerie glanced around to find the shooter, then narrowly pulled Robin and herself out of range before another shot nearly hit her. She had seen where it came from though—an upper ledge of the water reservoir, at least two figures.

"Hang tight," Valerie said, pulling Robin under a ledge and helping her put pressure on the wound. "It'll heal in no time, but just stay here. I'll take care of them and be right back."

"Punch him an extra time in the nuts for me before you kill him if it's a guy," Robin said.

"And if it's a girl?"

"Eh...same, but extra...hard." She flinched when her breathing sent a spasm through her. "Make sure...it fucking...hurts!"

"For you I'll bring the pain." Valerie almost leaned in to kiss her forehead, but instead clasped her shoulder, held her gaze for a moment, and took off at vampire speed. These little bastards were about to be dead, so she didn't care if they knew what she was capable of.

## Swarthian Extended Detention Environment (SEDE)

"If anyone asks," Etter told them as they walked the narrow passage between cell blocks, "I'm training you boys."

They'd left Kalan's mother's apartment over an hour ago and they'd spent the bulk of the intervening time in the kitchen with Etter, helping him prepare the food for the isolation wing's prisoners and loading it onto the cart.

Etter, it seemed, was the master of the art of preparing an impressively wide range of disgusting types of food. There was the gruel, which Kalan remembered all too well from his time inside. That would be for the Skulla and most other species. Pallicons preferred a gelatinous cube of a substance Kalan couldn't identify. It had strange purple specks floating in it that glowed, making Kalan wonder if it was even safe to be near it.

The final plate was a steaming pile of soft green plants that reminded Kalan of seaweed but smelled like rotting meat. He had no idea what species that disgusting mess was for, and he wasn't sure he wanted to find out.

Bob gave Etter a suspicious look. "They'll believe you're training us? Won't they check the records or something?"

Etter shrugged. "I have pretty free rein on who I bring aboard. As long as the food gets delivered, nobody dies, and everyone ends up in the correct cell at night, the Shimmers don't much care what I do."

After they'd been walking for a few more minutes, Bob grabbed Kalan's arm and fell behind Etter a few steps. He leaned over to Kalan. "Hey, where are you keeping your...you know?"

It took Kalan a moment, but then he realized Bob was talking about his pistol. He glanced down at Bob's right hand, where the man was unsuccessfully trying to keep his pistol up his sleeve without it slipping down. "I can see where you're keeping yours."

"Yeah, that's the problem, man. These prison uniforms weren't exactly designed for concealing a weapon, you know what I mean?"

"I think that's on purpose."

"So, any tips? I can't even see yours."

Kalan hesitated a moment before answering. "I don't have it. I left it with my mom."

Bob's jaw fell open. "Are you an idiot?"

"Probably, but if Zoras and his gang decide they want revenge, I don't want her unarmed. She's smart enough to keep it hidden and only use it if she absolutely needs to."

"You're a dedicated son. And she's some female."

Kalan frowned. "Don't think I didn't see the way you looked at her when we left."

"What can I say? I have a thing for females a foot taller than me."

Etter stopped at a heavy-duty steel door with a tiny window near the top. "This is us."

He waved his hand over a scanner next to the door and it chirped. The steel door slid open.

"Do you have a chip in your hand or something?" Bob asked.

Kalan grinned. "This is SEDE. *Everyone's* got a chip in their hand."

Etter gestured for them to step inside and pushed his food cart after them.

Kalan stopped a few feet past the door, taking in the oddity of the place. It was laid out exactly like the cell block on which he'd grown up, with one notable exception: there was only one apartment.

A single lonely little dwelling, surrounded by steel walls.

"Welcome to the isolation block, boys," Etter said with a smile. "The most dangerous, most hated, or most in need of protection call this home. You've either got to know powerful people or have done something truly awful to get thrown in here."

Bob whistled softly. "You been in here before, Kalan?"

Kalan shook his head. "I grew up hearing the stories,

though, so I always wanted to get a glimpse of it. All the worst stone-cold serial murderers in the system locked in one block. I gotta say, the reality is honestly a little underwhelming."

"It may not look like much," Etter said, "but every creature in it is here for a reason. Watch yourself. You may have bested Zoras, but even you don't want to mess with some of these guys."

"I'll take your word for that."

They followed Etter to the apartment. Even though the doors of all SEDE apartments were kept open during daylight hours, Etter knocked politely. A mild-looking Skulla answered the door and took the bowl of gruel from Etter while exchanging pleasantries.

As they walked away Bob whispered to the others, "He seemed nice. Is he a political prisoner or something?"

Etter chuckled. "That, my friend, was the Rainy-Day Killer."

"No kidding?" There was genuine surprise in Kalan's voice. He glanced at Bob and noticed his confusion. "He killed—what, thirty old ladies? Left their bodies in their gardens."

"But only on rainy days," Etter added. "Come on, there's much more work to do."

He ran his hand over the scanner at the far end of the room and they wheeled the cart into the next chamber. It was identical to the first.

They went on like that for the better part of an hour, delivering food to murderers, terrorists, and maniacs. Some were polite, like the Rainy-Day Killer. Others were surly and a few were downright angry, but they all had one thing in common: they wanted to spend a few minutes chatting with Etter.

In some cases the conversation involved yelling. In others it was mostly awkward silence. But in every case, Etter knew exactly how to handle it. He soothed, commiserated, or reprimanded, and each prisoner appeared satisfied with the interaction.

When they entered the fifteenth chamber of the isolation block, Etter turned to them and smiled. "This is it—the home of Sslake, former Minister of the Vurugu System."

Kalan drew a deep breath and looked at the apartment. It appeared identical to the others he'd seen, and yet the most popular politician of his lifetime lived here. He was the whole reason they'd come to SEDE.

As odd as it felt, he'd been enjoying making the rounds with Etter, but the fun times were over. It was time to get to work.

Etter approached and knocked, and a moment later a Skulla whose face Kalan had seen on a hundred digi-casts stepped into the doorway.

"Hello, Minister Sslake," Etter said.

The Skulla male waved a hand in front of him dismissively. "I've told you there's no need for formality, Etter. I'm simply 'Sslake' now."

Etter grinned. "You can keep correcting me, sir, but I'm going to keep saying it." He paused, then nodded toward Kalan and Bob. "You have some visitors, sir. I'm going to leave them with you while I complete the rest of my deliveries, then I'll swing back through. Sounds like they have something to discuss with you."

Sslake cast a discerning eye over Kalan and Bob. "I see. Very well, gentlemen. Would you like to come inside?"

"Yes, sir." Kalan stepped through the door, followed closely by Bob. When they were inside he spoke again. "Sir, my name is Kalan Grayhewn, and I've been sent here by friends. We need your help."

"Kalan," Bob said, his voice thick with urgency. "Something's not right. I hear—"

Before the human could finish something slammed into Kalan's chest, lifting him off his feet and driving him back. His crashed into the wall and hung there, his feet six inches off the ground.

From the pressure around his neck he knew someone had him by the throat, but he didn't see anyone in front of him.

There was only one explanation: it was a Shimmer.

Kalan tried to choke out a few words—anything to get this Shimmer to let go of him—but all that came out was a harsh croak.

Sslake stepped forward and stared up at Kalan, his eyes ice-cold. "This is my roommate Wearl. As you may have guessed, she's a Shimmer. She'd like to know who sent you to kill me."

## 18

**Planet Tol: The Water Plant**

The two attackers were running by the time Valerie reached them, but a third had been waiting to blast her as she came around the corner. Damn, the shots had hurt. Oddly the Skulla was using an old pellet gun loaded with tiny explosives. If Valerie hadn't dived to her left her face would've been full of holes instead of her arm getting peppered with pellets and one or two explosives.

*At least the fight will be fairer now*, she thought, grabbing the first attacker by the balls and tossing him over the railing to drop three stories.

She hoped that counted for Robin's request, but now she had her own pain to get them back for. Her eyes glowed red as she charged the next-closest one. This time she leaped sideways and rolled as soon as she heard the shot coming, so she felt only the heat of the little blasts.

When she came up the second Skulla was aiming a

trembling gun at her, his mouth moving as if he were praying.

"Who sent you?" she asked, snatching the gun out of his hands and backhanding him. She ducked down beside him, using the edge of one of the support beams for cover from the third shooter, and asked again. "Who the fuck sent you?"

He spat blood and mouthed "Wandrei," which Valerie was beginning to understand was much more of an insult than she had originally thought, then tried to punch her.

She grabbed the fist and twisted until the wrist snapped, and then smiled. "Ah, your joints *do* work like ours."

While his face turned red he tried to lunge at her, teeth bared and lips curled as if he were going to bite her.

Her response was an open palm to the nose. That sent him reeling backward, where he fell, twitched, and was still.

One more, and that meant only one more chance to find out who was behind this. Was it random, this planet's equivalent of terrorists or rogue actors? She doubted it.

"Lower your weapon and come baring your soul," she shouted to the third, "and maybe we can both walk out of here alive."

A shot answered her.

*Fine.* She had left her sword on the ship, as it would have been too obvious to carry here, but she had concealed a small pistol. She drew it now, charging toward him and blasting at foot-level.

The Skulla pulled back and leaped behind a rock, but that had been her intent. He hadn't known how fast she was, and by the time he had recovered she had advanced and pressed her gun to his head.

"Tell me everything and you get to die." Her finger was on the trigger, ready to display his brains. "Who?"

"Go home! You're not welcome here." The male tried to struggle but she kicked him back down, still holding the pistol so that she could take his life at any minute. Her other arm was burning, but she knew the healing effects would kick in soon; it was all temporary. "Who was behind this?"

He was half-turned to her and she leaned in, letting him see her red eyes. She *pushed* fear, though she wasn't sure it would be effective.

Against a human or Were or even other vampires, it had worked wonders. On this Skulla it had a different effect. He suddenly calmed, and then began blabbing.

"The Bandian, he tries to keep foreigners out of the contest. He makes moves on them before the fight. Sometimes they make it and enter, and that's fine—they've got to be damn tough to survive both an attack like this and the Damu Michezo, especially since they're usually wounded in the attack."

"So *that's* the game," she said, relaxing slightly. Then she frowned, guard back up. "Why are you telling me this?"

He suddenly looked worried and shook his head. "Wh- what did you do to me?"

It was possible that he was faking it, but she decided to try again. *Pushing* fear, she asked, "What's the most embarrassing thing that's ever happened to you?"

Again his eyes took on a distant look and he replied, "I shat myself the first day on the job for Noru, a warlord I used to work for. Everyone smelled it, but I tried to deny it was me until it started seeping out of my pants. It would've been less horrible if I hadn't had to waddle home. Ran into the female of my dreams on the way."

"Oh, damn." Valerie stared in disgust, then started laughing. "That's pretty bad."

His face took on a horrified expression and he glanced at her, scared. He stuttered, "How the... How the h-h-hell did you do that?"

She *pushed* fear again. "Seems I have a built-in truth serum with your race. Weird, but let's have fun with it. What's the best way forward from here?"

"Go on as you were, enter the fight, and hope your injury doesn't get you killed." His eyes flickered to her arm and she grunted.

"Right, I'll have to have that looked at. And you? Are you going to attack me again if I let you live?"

His eyes narrowed, then took on that distant look again as she *pushed* fear harder. "No," he replied. "Not as long as you break my legs or something." Panic flashed across his face and he started to yell, "Don't do tha—"

But it was too late. She had lifted a leg in an axe-stomp and brought the heel of her boot down hard on his ankle. They both heard the loud *crack*.

His grunts of pain were mixed with swear words as he struggled to pull himself toward his fallen gun. Valerie stepped forward and kicked it over the ledge, and then gave him a friendly nod.

"Hey, thanks for the info. And you know, don't forget that I spared you if the chance should ever come your way to do the same."

As she walked away he shouted after her, "Right after I break every bone in your damned body!"

She shrugged, because yeah, while that would suck, she would likely heal from it. There had been a time when pain had almost terrified her. It still pissed her off and she didn't like it, but she'd take it over death any day, now that she knew her purpose in this universe.

When she found Robin, the woman was massaging her wound. It had started healing nicely, and would likely be done by the time they reached Warlord Palnik's mansion.

They went the rest of the way together in peace, complaining and laughing about their injuries. Robin especially liked the part when Valerie had grabbed the guy by the balls to throw him.

"Don't get me wrong, I respect the family jewels," she said, "but after a bastard tries to shoot me it's over. No more respect."

"Right. A guy tries to kill a lady, I'd say that nullifies his rights to offspring."

Robin laughed, then grimaced in pain as she held her injury and took a breather.

They rested for a moment, ignoring the glances of a few passersby, and then continued the rest of the way. Valerie was surprised to see what looked like a little procession in front of the mansion.

While most Skulla wore clothes that didn't stand out as crazy, this group was an exception. They had larger heads than normal too, and Valerie had to assume they'd had brain modifications. Around their heads were wreaths of red and blue metal adorned with shiny stones in a pattern that resembled the stars. Each wore a long silver cloak with the hood down, except for the one in the middle. She had her hood up, but it only covered the back half of her head. Beneath the open robes they wore an assortment of blues and reds, with sashes and all.

Valerie glanced at her companion and saw that Robin was doing her damnedest not to laugh.

"This ought to be fun," Robin said.

"Maybe for you," Valerie replied. "I'm the one who's going to be kissing their asses."

"Kiss asses today to kick asses tomorrow."

"Shut up." Valerie ignored the corny wink, strolling forward to see what this was about.

As she approached she saw that it wasn't only this oddly dressed group in the courtyard. Warlord Palnik and several of his guards were there as well, sitting in their midst and sharing some sort of steaming beverage with an old female. The hooded female stood at her back, eyes moving to Valerie and Robin as they approached.

"That will be close enough, Wandrei," she said.

Valerie paused, wondering what would happen if she continued to walk forward. They might attack, and then she'd have to kill them all... Not her goal here, so she stayed put.

"Ah, my champion made it!" Palnik announced, and stood with a smile and outstretched arms. "Oh, no, you're injured! I trust you still wish to proceed?"

"I do."

Nothing about his expression gave away any knowledge of the attack on the way over, but Valerie had a good notion he knew.

A glance at her arm showed it was mostly healed, and

when she turned to Robin she saw that hers was the same. Their clothes were torn and singed more than made sense considering their wounds, but no one seemed to need an explanation.

"We want a chance at citizenship," Valerie offered, "same as everyone else."

"And yet," the female seated opposite Palnik stood, "you are nothing like everyone else. You are from the Etheric Federation, no?" She was short and slender, her braids adorned with those shiny stones and interwoven with the colored metal.

A hint of cold seemed to roll off the female at the mention of the Etheric Federation, so Valerie decided to wing it.

"Exiles, ma'am. We saw their expansion, we challenged it. Now we're seeking a fresh start here."

"Is that so?" the female turned to them, hands behind her back, and asked, "Your letter of introduction?"

Valerie presented the disk. Nothing in the female's expression conveyed surprise or boredom at the exchange as she accepted it. She checked the disk in a holo-display built into an advanced mechanical contraption on her arm. Now that Valerie looked closely, she saw that beneath the robes there were several bulging areas that hinted at the possibility of other such contraptions. She wondered what they were capable of; what sort of technology this group might have that those from Earth still lacked.

"Everything seems in order," the female said, touching two fingers to her forehead in what Valerie figured was similar to a handshake or a bow. "Welcome to the Damu Michezo."

## Swarthian Extended Detention Environment (SEDE)

Kalan clawed at the invisible hand holding his throat to no avail; the Shimmer would not be letting go anytime soon. The hand was pressing hard, making breathing difficult and speaking impossible.

For once Kalan was glad he had Bob on his side.

"Kill you?" Bob shouted at the politician. "Are you fucking serious right now? We're not here to kill you! We're here to *rescue* you."

Sslake kept his eyes fixed on Kalan. "That seems unlikely. Two men do not a rescue party make."

"It does when those two men are awesome!" Bob countered. He paused for a moment, staring at the apparently occupied spot in front of Kalan. "And you! Watch your mouth, you invisible bastard. Kalan's my friend. I know his breath is not the greatest, but we've been trying to break in here for the past day and a half, so he hasn't had a chance to brush his teeth."

For the first time Sslake's cool demeanor waivered. "Hold on, you can hear her?"

Bob's eyes narrowed. "That thing's a girl? You're shacking up with a girl Shimmer?"

"Not like that," Sslake snapped. He sighed. "Wearl, let him down please. Let's hear what they have to say."

To Kalan's great relief the fingers around his neck loosened and he collapsed to the floor, gasping for air. After a moment, he struggled to his feet and wiped the tears from his eyes.

"As my friend said," Kalan croaked hoarsely, "we're here

to rescue you."

Sslake frowned. "I see. And your big plan was to get arrested and sentenced to SEDE? What's Step Two?"

"We're not big planners," Bob said.

Kalan ignored the comment. "We weren't arrested, sir. We snuck aboard a transport carrying contraband. He's Bob, and my name's Kalan. I'm a former inmate here."

Sslake looked surprised at that. "Why in the dusty hells would you come back here voluntarily?"

"Because we need you." Kalan took a deep breath. He knew this next part was important. He needed to get Sslake on board quickly so they could get moving. "Things are bad out there, Minister. The Bandian is extorting beings dry with his various protection schemes. The only chance most people have of moving up in society is the fighting pits, and that usually means death. Economies are crumbling, and war is on the horizon."

For a moment Sslake looked like he was going to argue, but then he sighed and sank onto the concrete bench near the door. "Nobir. I've known him since long before he started calling himself 'the Bandian.' Since before he was a warlord, even. I'd been busting him for his illegal genetic experiments for years, but I underestimated him."

"It's not your fault, sir," Kalan said.

Sslake grimaced. "How a former SEDE prisoner is qualified to determine that I do not know, but thank you." He thought for a moment. "Say you're right. Say that against all odds you somehow manage to get me out of here. The Bandian is still in charge, right? I don't want to live my life on the run. I might as well stay here."

"We have friends working on taking down the Bandian."

"Who?"

Kalan exchanged a glance with Bob. "A covert team operating under orders from the Etheric Federation."

Sslake sat up a bit straighter. "Ah, that's your game. Save me and I'm in your debt, is that it? You'll get a political ally?"

Bob answered before Kalan could. "We just want to do what's right, sir."

Sslake shrugged. "I doubt you're as noble as all that. Still, I never had a problem with the Etheric Federation. I've heard the scary stories about their queen like everybody else, but I don't believe them. As far as I can tell they have been a force for good in the galaxy. I simply wasn't ready to join them."

Kalan nodded slowly. "Honestly, sir, I couldn't give two shits about the Etheric Federation, but I know the good you did in office and I'd like to do my part to put you back there."

Bob tilted his head a moment. "Wearl says that's a sensible approach."

A high-pitched bell near the door rang.

"Ha!" Sslake laughed. "I guess you really *can* hear her. Look." He pointed at two bells dangling from strings on the wall, one twice the size of the other. "We had to devise a method of basic communication and that's what we came up with. She rings the small bell for yes and the larger one for no."

The smaller bell tinkled again.

"How'd you end up with a roommate, sir?" Kalan asked.

"This is the isolation block. Isn't the whole point for you to be segregated?"

Sslake smiled. "Theoretically. The truth is, Wearl took a liking to me and the other Shimmers couldn't figure out how to keep her away. From what I've been able to determine through yes and no questions, the other Shimmers think she's crazy. I guess she killed a couple of them. They tried to put her in gen pop, but she made her way here. Isn't that right?"

The small bell rang.

"She also says she likes your politics," Bob added.

Sslake let out a full-throated laugh. "You're going to be handy to have around, friend. You've figured out more about her in five minutes than I have in two years. So seriously, what's the plan? I'm not saying I'll go with you, but if I did?"

Kalan thought a moment before answering. "We wait for Etter to come back through. When he does, he'll take us out into the restricted area, and from there, we make our way to our ride and fly back to Tol."

Sslake raised an eyebrow. "Your ride? You have a way out of here?"

He willed Bob not to speak as he answered, "We do." It was only a partial lie. They didn't have a ride, but he was pretty sure he knew how they could get one.

"Look, I'm not trying to be self-important here," Sslake said, "but from the guards' perspective I'm the most valuable prisoner in SEDE. The Bandian commanded them to keep me locked up and alive. He doesn't want me to be a martyr, and he certainly doesn't want me running free. He wants to break me, and then announce I'm alive and make me publicly support him. What I'm saying is, I'm going to need a little more than 'We have a ride'."

Kalan looked him in the eye. "You have my word I'm going to get you out of here. Right now that's all I can give you."

"Huh," Sslake grunted. "So Etter just walks us out of the isolation block?"

Bob nodded. "He's got that hand-chip-thing. Opens these doors."

Sslake stared at Bob a moment, then the color drained from his face. "Oh, you idiots. You absolute fools."

Bob and Kalan looked at each, both confused.

"What is it?" Kalan asked.

"You said you're a former inmate, right? That means you have a SEDE chip implant."

"Sure," Kalan agreed, "but I didn't use it."

Sslake shook his head in disbelief. "You don't *have* to use them. The chips aren't only for opening doors, they're for tracking inmates. If you have the chip, they've been tracking you since the moment you stepped into the cell block. They know you're here. They have to."

Kalan shook his head. Was that even possible?

"Damn it all," Bob exclaimed. "You said it yourself, Kalan. All SEDE prisoners have chips implanted."

"I don't believe it," Kalan said. "Why would they do that? Why didn't they take me down the moment they discovered me?"

Bob listened for a moment, then said, "Wearl thinks they wanted to know your plan. What you were after. Now that they know, they should be descending on you and tearing you to shreds at any moment."

"Thanks, Wearl. Okay, look, if that really is the case then we have to get ready. Prepare for a fight."

"Wearl says it's too late." Bob's voice trembled when he spoke. "She can sense the other Shimmers, and they're coming. Now."

A silence hung over the room for a long moment. This was it—Kalan had failed. The full force of the guards of SEDE was about to descend on him and Bob. They were as good as dead.

Thinking they could rescue Minister Sslake had been foolish. Pure hubris, through and through. And assuming he could waltz into the most secure prison in the galaxy? Of course they had *let* him walk in. He was an idiot to have thought otherwise.

The only thing more foolish was the assumption that he'd be able to walk out of SEDE with their most important prisoner. The one they'd do anything to protect...

Kalan looked up sharply. "Bob, give me your pistol."

"Uh, I don't think so. I'm not the one who gave mine to my mommy. If there's a fight coming—"

"Would you trust me and hand it over?"

Reluctantly Bob pulled the pistol from his sleeve and handed it to Kalan.

"Thank you." Kalan rose and walked to the door. "Minister, do you mind coming here a moment?"

Sslake did as he asked, stepping onto the crumbling landing with Kalan.

They waited for only a few moments before the door at the far end of the room opened. Kalan didn't see anyone come through, but the door stayed open for a long time.

"Are they here?" he asked.

"Yeah," Bob answered. "They're here, and they are *not* happy."

"Good." Kalan threw an arm around Sslake's neck and pulled the minister in front of him.

"What are you doing?" Sslake asked, his voice alive with panic.

"Shut up," Kalan replied. He pressed the barrel of Bob's pistol into the minister's temple, then spoke in a loud voice to the invisible throng in front of him. "I need everyone to stay very still. Any of you Shimmer bastards puts one see-through foot on this landing, I blow Sslake's brains out."

**Planet Tol: the Fighting Arena**

Valerie had been assigned a room at the stadium, where she had spent the pre-fight hours stretching, meditating, and being briefed on the rules.

Early rounds of the Damu Michezo were generally fought hand-to-hand, without armor. Those who chose to advance in their quest for glory, titles, and power would see the use of armor and weapons. But later.

They had given her an outfit that fit oddly and was much too small. She didn't want to think about the dark stains at key points or wonder how many fighters had died in these very clothes.

While the streets were mostly full of Skulla, the arena's fighter halls were full of various other alien races, though she only caught glances. At one point she thought she saw the backside of an upright rhino, but didn't want to make it awkward by running over to have a look.

"I would ask if you're ready," Garcia said, leaning out

the window and watching the crowds gather, "but you being Valerie, I'm not worried."

"Neither am I," Valerie replied, wondering if they bought it. While she was confident in her abilities, the unknown had always given her more unease than anything else. She could be facing off against the devil himself and not be too worried as long as she knew what she was up against.

Here, anything was possible.

Robin, however, approached the wall and leaned close so that only Valerie could see her face. She gave her a concerned look before whispering, "Are you sure?"

Valerie nodded, turning to the group again. "Whatever happens out there, we know this: I can heal from a damn lot. So can you all, after the mods. Robin's a crazy assassin, Garcia's this badass sergeant who could take down an entire base by himself even without the mods, and Flynn... Well, I don't know much about you, actually, Flynn, but you're buff and tall. That's gotta at least intimidate them."

"I can hold my own," the corporal said with a laugh. "Just can't stand toe to toe with Garcia here. You sell him short—a base? I'd be willing to put money on him taking down this whole planet if we unleashed him."

"Might not be any survivors when I was done," Garcia replied with a barking laugh, "but you tell me to do it, I get it done."

Flynn nodded, clasping the sergeant's shoulder. "Point proven, badass."

"What *is* your story anyway?" Robin asked Flynn, turning to him now. "I mean, if TH put his trust in you there must've been a reason."

"Colonel Walton? I didn't serve with him long, but I think he saw loyalty in me." Flynn stood tall and proud. "It's what I'm known for, or was, in the crews I ran with before the colonel."

"I'll take loyal over many other qualities," Valerie admitted. "And don't sell yourself short—I saw you fight. Just because this beast beat you," she jerked a thumb in Garcia's direction, "doesn't mean you aren't a fighter."

His mouth curled in a smile and Valerie felt something sappy coming on, so she cleared her throat and turned back to Robin.

"Okay, throw one at me."

"What?" Robin asked.

"A punch. You know, to warm me up." She shook her limbs and took a defensive stance.

The other two stepped back, and Robin smiled and came in with a vampiric-speed punch. It nearly caught Valerie but she moved her head just out of its trajectory, an inch away from the fist, and then slammed her palm against the arm, knocking her friend off balance.

"Not bad, but make me work for it."

Robin came in with a fake kick this time, transitioning to a superman punch and then a one-two and a spinning backhand.

Valerie caught them all, but the follow-on hip-check knocked her into the side punch Robin threw. The pain lasted only a moment, then was healed.

"Let's hope I'm not facing vampires out there," Valerie said with a chuckle, rubbing the spot to ensure it was back to normal. "Now you, Flynn."

He stared at her, mouth open.

"Come on! I need a variety of styles to deal with," she said. "What if I go up against an octopus or something?"

"I'm an octopus?" he asked.

"Hardly. At the moment you're more like a slug. Now hit me."

He cocked his head, clearly torn about something.

"What is it?" she asked.

"It's just... I don't hit women." Everyone started cracking up at that, except for Flynn, who plaintively asked, "What? I don't. Why's that funny?"

"You dolt," Garcia said, wiping away a tear of laughter. "It's funny that you think you have a shot of actually hitting her."

That pissed Flynn off and he charged forward. To his credit his style was quite different from Robin's, going for the giant's versus the little person's approach of trying to clobber or grab her.

To her surprise, in his next attack he came in with a knee, followed by a spinning round-kick that nearly took her in the head. She swept the leg, grabbing him as he fell to spin him around and catch him in an armlock.

"Not a bad try, though," Valerie admitted, helping him up.

"Where the hell did those moves come from?" Garcia asked, impressed.

As Valerie let Flynn up he replied, "This old man when I was growing up taught me a thing or two. Called it 'Muay Thai.'"

"I like this Mai Tai stuff," Robin said with a raised brow. "Maybe you have a thing or two to show us while Valerie's out there getting her ass handed to her."

"*Muay* Thai," Flynn corrected, "and sure."

"You want me to have a go?" Garcia asked Valerie. "I mean, you feeling warmed up, or you want more?"

Valerie felt the pump of her blood, the sense of being ready for anything, and shook her head. "Save your energy. We don't know what I'll face."

"Roger that."

Valerie turned to the array of food Garcia and Flynn had managed to arrange and took a swig of what she supposed passed for water. She followed it up with some local nuts, which were almost red in color and tasted similar to what she imagined dirt tasted like. They'd have to do.

"When this is over..." Robin started, looking around at them, "what do you think comes next?"

"You mean when we've gotten our intel and checked in with the colonel?" Flynn asked.

She shook her head. "When the Etheric Federation has won. What then? Go back home and live life on Earth as if none of this exists?"

"Val?" Garcia asked, apparently noticing the scrunched-up look she now realized her face had taken on. "What is it?"

"I don't know that the war could ever really be over. How vast is this universe? We have gateways, but how do we know how many other gateways there could be?"

"You're saying the war might never be over," Robin said, blowing a breath out. "Damn! I mean, you're probably right, but... *Damn*."

She nodded. "That said, if anyone wants to go back to Earth I imagine there's a way."

"Forget that," Robin replied. "You're here, I'm here. That's how it works."

"Same goes for me," Garcia added.

"Loyalty." Flynn pounded his chest. "I'm in it to win it."

Valerie nodded, glancing through the stone window at the sky. Orange clouds swirled overhead. "And this Kalan guy? And Bob? Where do they fit into this?"

"Bob's a bit of a turd, but…" Garcia wrinkled his nose, "I like him. Flynn, what do you think? You're Mr. Loyalty, you say, so what's your loyalty radar say about him?"

"Like you said, a turd," Flynn replied, staring off in thought for a moment. "Sometimes a giant, stinky, maybe even moldy turd, but I'd say he's *our* turd to the bitter end."

"Kalan seems trustworthy," Valerie added. "Wouldn't have sent Bob with him otherwise, and yeah, I'm glad you all say so—although now I wonder what you call me behind my back. If he's a turd, I'm…what? A harpy? Crazy pile of bat brains? A sour witch's teat?"

Garcia chuckled nervously, but waved her off. "You're giving me good ideas, but shit, boss—you gotta earn that stuff. You haven't been half as badass as all that."

"Fine, I'll work on it. Increase my bitchiness a bit. I kinda like the sound of 'Harpy Hag,' if you ever decide on a moniker. It's insulting, and yet it speaks to my level of intimidation, you know?"

"You've got issues," Robin replied, then laughed, shaking her head. "'Harpy Hag?' You're more like a mother lion."

"Doesn't have the same ring to it."

A loud drum started banging, echoing through the halls under the arena. It was time.

As many times as Valerie had been in these situations, it still caused a flutter in her heart. She had even fought in an arena before, in Toro, and a different type of fighting competition in the bazaar when New York had still been Old Manhattan—before she'd helped build it back up. Considering that she was on an alien planet and in a completely different situation, it still felt like the first time.

"Let's crack some skulls," she said, then took a breath and headed for the door.

---

**Swarthian Extended Detention Environment (SEDE)**

"Kalan, what are you doing?" Bob hissed. He paused a moment, then added, "No, Wearl, I don't think you should rip his head off. Hold on."

Kalan kept his eyes focused on the seemingly empty area in front of him where he knew the Shimmers were gathered. He said through gritted teeth, "I know what I'm doing. Wearl, you can see the other Shimmers, right?"

"She says she can," Bob answered.

"Good. How many are there?"

A long pause, then Bob passed along her reply. "About thirty. Also, she says she's looking forward to watching them dismember you."

"Well, I'm glad to know my final moments will bring someone pleasure." Despite his bravado, Kalan wasn't entirely sure this would work. All he knew was the Shimmers had come to stop them, and that Sslake was the most valuable prisoner in SEDE. If Sslake died at the hands of an ex-con who wasn't even supposed to be there, the Shimmers would have some serious explaining to do to their bosses.

He hoped that was enough to buy him a little time to figure out what to do next. As much as he hated to admit it, he didn't have a grand plan.

"Wearl says they're creeping closer," Bob announced.

"Back up!" Kalan shouted. "Just because you're invisible doesn't mean we can't see what you're up to."

Sslake cleared his throat and spoke in a calm, quiet voice. "Kalan, if I might offer a suggestion?"

"Uh, yeah, of course. Sorry about this, by the way."

"Perfectly understandable," the minister answered. He spoke softly so that only Kalan could hear him. "It seems to me you may not have thought this through. Now that you've taken me hostage, you need to commit. I take it you know your way around SEDE?"

Kalan hesitated. "More or less."

"And I have no doubt you can fight, so here's what we do. Tell them you will let me go once you are at your ride. You don't want to free me anymore, you simply want to get out of here alive. Understand where I'm going with this?"

Kalan nodded slowly. "Yeah, actually I think I do." He wasn't sure the idea would work, but it was sort of brilliant in a crazy way. A lot of things would have to go right in order for this to work, but he was already running through the possible outcomes in his mind. "We want them to take us to the Nim hangar. If we can get there and buy ourselves a few minutes, I think I can get us out of here."

"Good. The Shimmers' understanding of human speech is not the most nuanced, so we'll need some assistance handling the negotiation portion." In a louder voice he said, "Wearl, would you come here please?"

The minister then quietly explained the plan to Wearl. "Now, would you please negotiate how many guards they'll be sending to escort us? We'd like to keep that number as low as possible, obviously."

Kalan waited, the barrel of the pistol still against Sslake's head, as the tension mounted. A lot would depend on what happened next.

Bob put his hands over his ears. "Ah! They're all shouting."

"What are they saying?" Kalan asked.

"I don't know. They're talking too quickly, and I can't fully process. There're a lot of threats. Vivid description of how they will desecrate each other's corpses."

"Standard Shimmer negotiation tactics," Sslake pointed out.

Another moment and it was over.

"Okay," Bob announced. "They've reached an agreement. Seven Shimmers will escort us to the Nim hangar."

"Seven?" Sslake sounded disappointed. "That'll be difficult."

"But it's possible." In reality Kalan wasn't so sure, but he wanted to be hopeful.

"One more thing," Sslake said quietly. "For this to work, they need to be convinced I don't want to go with you. At some point before we leave this room I'm going to try to break free, and you need to hit me. Understand?"

Kalan grimaced. Punching the rightful leader of the Vurugu system wasn't high on his to do list, but if it had to be done, so be it.

"Wearl, are they clearing a path for us?" It felt odd talking to an invisible creature, but since she was the only one who could see the other Shimmers he didn't have much of a choice.

"They are," Bob replied. "Wearl says to head straight down the center. They'll move out of your way."

"You ready, Minister?" Kalan asked in a whisper.

"To get out of here? Very much so."

Kalan smiled for the first time since leaving his mom's house. "Okay, then. Here we go."

The first step into the passage was the most difficult. He'd grown up with tales of the Shimmers that might as well have been ghost stories. Yarns about prisoners taken in the night, a Pallicon female who dared to breathe a negative word about one of the guards and immediately fell dead, shot by a Shimmer she didn't know was standing behind her. And his personal favorite, the Skulla male who'd attempted escape, not knowing he was surrounded by Shimmers throughout the entire process. He only found out when one of them removed his scalp with an invisible blade.

Come to think of it, that last one struck a little too close to home.

He didn't know which of the stories were true and which weren't. The fact was, even though he'd grown up here, he'd had very little contact with the Shimmers. They only intervened when there was trouble, and while he'd caused his fair share of trouble, he'd also been very good at avoiding being caught.

Besides, he'd had enough to worry about from beings like Zoras who wanted to take control and lord their power over their fellow prisoners. He hadn't had the energy left over at the end of the day to worry much about Shimmers.

And yet here he was, standing in a room full of them. He couldn't see the guards, but he knew every one of them wanted him dead. He'd committed the ultimate sin one could perpetrate aboard SEDE: he'd made them look bad.

He crept along slowly and carefully, one arm around Sslake's throat, the other holding the pistol to the minister's head.

When they were halfway across the room the politician tensed, and Kalan knew it was time. Sslake was making his move.

Kalan loosened his grip ever so slightly and Sslake took advantage, moving surprisingly quickly for a middle-aged politician. He wriggled out of Kalan's grasp.

Kalan knew he couldn't afford to hesitate even for a moment. If the Shimmers got hold of Sslake this was over, so he drew back a fist and let loose, catching Sslake in the eye with a solid punch.

The minister cried out in pain. The act might have been planned, but that cry wasn't fake. Kalan pushed down the feelings of guilt leaping into his chest and once again grabbed Sslake around the neck. Then he cast a wild gaze around the room, glaring at the guards he couldn't see.

"Stay the hell back!" he ordered. "If one of you so much as breathes on me I'll kill Sslake."

"Wearl says they're staying back," Bob told them softly.

"Good. Very good." Then, in a whisper, "You all right, Minister?"

Sslake groaned. "I said to punch me, not to hit me in the face with a rocket."

"Sorry. Tried to make it look real."

When they reached the door Kalan paused and a moment later the door slid open, the scanner apparently having been activated by one of the guards.

Kalan stepped through, then muttered over his shoulder, "Wearl, make sure no more than seven follow us through."

"She's on it," Bob said.

They made their way through the rest of the isolation block at a painfully slow pace, stopping at each door and waiting for a guard to open it. Wearl checked each room they entered to make sure there weren't Shimmers waiting to jump them.

Eventually they made it out and Kalan took a hard right out of the isolation block, happy to be back in familiar territory.

They proceeded down a long, broad corridor. Kalan was closer to his goal now, but he didn't dare relax.

Soon they would reach the Nim hangar, and that was where the real fun would begin.

## Planet Tol: the Fighting Arena

Valerie wasn't the first to fight, and that annoyed her as much as it relieved her. She had to stand with an array of stinky fighters in this barred and spiked pit and watch others get their asses handed to them.

A ceremony had started the day's fights, and Valerie learned through the whispers around her that they were an ongoing thing; there were always fights. Their way of entertaining themselves, it seemed. Their lives revolved around work and this. One Skulla had lived here for years, but had recently had a baby and therefore finally decided his family needed citizenship. A female was in a similar situation, but she had two kids and a mate who had left for another planet in search of wealth and never returned, so she had decided it was her turn to look for a way to upgrade their station in life.

All of it was so sad, and yet when the music started and dancers moved across the fighting pit kicking up sand and waving their silks, she felt as if she too were part of it all. She could almost taste the excitement of the crowd, as well as the anticipation of the people around her. This wasn't about a fight to the death for most of them. It was a chance at a better life for themselves and their loved ones.

If they died, where did that leave those loved ones? She had to assume the local authorities had distributed their fair share of propaganda to kick this idea out of their minds.

The first fighter was one she hadn't spoken with—a non-Skulla, or 'Wandrei' as she now began to think of them and herself.

"Let the fighting commence!" The booming voice echoed through the arena, and Valerie had to lean down to get a good view of the crowds. Even then she couldn't see everyone, there were so many. She wasn't sure she had ever seen this many beings in one place before, even back home in Capital Square.

The fighters jockeyed around, each trying to test the other, clearly not experienced at this.

When one moved to punch the other but hesitated at the last minute and backed up instead, a voice said, "Too slow!" and an electric shock ran across the floor, sending both to their knees in pain.

Cheers rose from the crowd and some even threw rocks at them, though none hit.

"That's barbaric," Valerie protested, slamming her hand against the wall in her fury.

"It's part of the game," the female Skulla to her right said. "We've all seen it. We've been briefed. And it works…look."

She gestured to the fight, and Valerie saw that it had indeed lit the needed fire under their asses. The fighters had charged in and were throwing haymakers and a weird barrage of clearly unskilled assaults.

"This isn't good," the female Skulla said.

"What's that?"

"Judges know that will take too long, or that the fighters will grow tired. Not a good show."

"So they'll intervene," Valerie said as the realization came. "That's not just."

"It's about keeping the people in line," the male Skulla said. "Give them entertainment, satiate their thirst for blood." He eyed her and she had a feeling he knew more than he was letting on. "You give the general populace this while giving them a chance to escape the dull, pitiful lives they live, you have won—which means the rest of us have lost."

Valerie shook her head. "Nobody's won yet. That's why I'm here."

"Okay," he replied with a grunt.

The female Skulla though, waited a second, and then pulled Valerie aside. After a quick look around she leaned in and said, "There are those among the Skulla who'd agree."

"Hmm?"

"About nobody having won. They want to rise but need a beacon, a symbol of victory. You could be that symbol."

Valerie leaned in, lowering her voice. "What are you talking about exactly? Rebellion?"

The Skulla nodded.

Valerie glanced around, noticing the guards in the back,

a couple of strange-looking alien fighters on the far side of the room, and various modified Skulla.

"How many are we talking about here?" she asked.

The Skulla furrowed her brow. "All."

"What do you mean?"

"I mean, if they had the right leader, I can't think of a single citizen who wouldn't rise against the system. Well, of course the elites might prefer the current system, but even among them there are the corrupt. They volunteered to get where they are, after all."

Valerie considered that for a moment. The idea of death and where murder put one on the moral scale was tough, considering all that she had done in the name of justice or on her new mission in the universe. But that was different —it didn't have personal gain as the motive behind it, at least not for her. She couldn't be sure how often she had been used, or when the moral line was grayer than not.

"Wait a minute," Valerie hissed. "You're in here."

The Skulla glanced around again. "Not by choice."

Valerie's eyes went wide. She wanted to ask many questions, but at that moment the others started yelling about weapons.

Everyone dashed over to the viewing area, pushing Valerie and the Skulla with them, so she went with it, determined to find time to ask later.

Sure enough, several stands with weapons had risen out of the ground in the arena and one of the fighters had already grabbed a crude-looking sword. Its blade was bent and had three vertical points coming out the side. Perhaps a local tool?

He charged the other, who was running for a weapon

that closely resembled a baseball bat. Unfortunately for him, he didn't make it.

The next part was gruesome and Valerie had to turn away. Not because she was disgusted by the blood by any means, but because she was disgusted by the crowd's reactions. Cheers erupted with each stab, again and again.

"If you're talking about them," Valerie said to the female Skulla between cheers, leaning close to her ear, "I don't think you're reading the situation right."

"Anyone who shows a lack of excitement is assumed to be a dissenter and...removed."

"Removed," Valerie repeated the word, hating what it meant.

It was clear this planet wouldn't be an optimal Federation ally, at least not as it currently stood.

As of that moment, this fight was no longer about simply earning favor to get intel. It became about making a difference. Overthrowing the system, if possible. And she was sick of watching and listening.

Pushing past the guards, she strode into the fighting pit. The guards followed her, but there in the seat of honor, high above the arena, was the female with the gems in her hair, her attendants nearby. At a wave from the female, the guards stopped pursuing.

"I want the best," Valerie shouted. "Give me your champion and I'll give you a show!"

The crowd was silent for a moment from pure shock. Then like thunder breaking they cheered, many pounding their feet.

Another wave from the female shut them up, and she stood. "That is not how things are done here, Wandrei."

Complete silence again.

"These fine Skulla came for a show. They want blood? Well, what better way to give it to them than from the lips of a vampire?"

With that Valerie ran forward and leaped from one of the weapon stands. She hit the rail of the stands and ran along it, *pushing* fear and letting her eyes glow red as she went. When she was at the seat of honor she froze, snarling so that her fangs showed.

It was a gamble—a show of force and power—and she had no idea how it would be received.

"If you won't give it to me, I'll take it," she said and smiled, pulling one of the guards with her as she jumped back into the pit. It was a long drop, but one she was ready for.

As she hit she pushed off from the guard, letting him take the majority of the impact as she rolled aside.

When she'd recovered she turned to see him struggling to stand, but then he collapsed.

"Your champion is defeated," Valerie proclaimed. "I'll be back tomorrow for a real fight."

Before they could respond or try to do anything that might actually threaten her, Valerie darted at vampire speed into the stands, making it out through the windows and clawing her way down.

She could only hope Robin and the others would have the wisdom to head back and not get trapped themselves. To be sure, she lingered right outside the main part of the city until she saw movement.

It wasn't them, though, but one of the city's small fighters. She started running, debating whether she could take it down or not, and was just about to speed up when the door opened and Robin's face poked out.

"Get in, you idiot," she shouted, and the fighter dropped.

"You took one of their fighters?" Valerie asked. She jumped for it, landing inside as the ramp raised. "What if they have a tracker? Won't that lead them to us?"

"That was the plan, actually," Garcia said, pointing to Flynn. "We fly it out a ways, then double back to the *Grandeur*. Lead them off our path."

"Not bad, actually," Valerie said, catching her breath.

"Sure, not bad if we stick to the plan," Robin shouted. "Some of us are capable of that, but others are…less so!"

Valerie glanced at them, furious that they should second-guess her, but then her head started to clear. Damn! Maybe she had made a mistake?

Had she acted rashly? Clearly Robin felt she had.

"It… It'll work out," Valerie said, moving to the wall. She plopped down and rested her head against it, and closed her eyes.

Fuck, she hoped it really *would* work out and she hadn't just screwed up her very first mission for Bad Company and the Etheric Federation. If she'd ruined it, she would have come here for nothing. Robin would have left her parents behind for nothing.

And whatever existed of this rebellion? Nothing would come of it, most likely.

"Hell, no," she said, eyes popping open. She stood again, determined. "I made the right call, dammit, and tomorrow I'm going to prove it to you."

The others stared at her in shock, then Robin nodded.

The fighter swerved as Garcia looked back and Flynn shrugged.

"Good! I hope so," Flynn shrugged, "because honestly, that was *awesome!*"

Valerie smiled, and the rest started laughing and agreeing, telling her where they had been at the time, the feelings of shock and awe that had hit them as they saw what she was doing, and how they had gotten out of there by tackling a couple guards who were trying to intercept her.

Even Robin was into it now that her initial bout of anger had passed.

Sure, it was going to be insane from here out, but that only made it more fun. And tomorrow they were going to fucking *bring* it.

**Swarthian Extended Detention Environment (SEDE)**

As they approached the Nim hangar, Kalan leaned over to Bob. "I need Wearl. Tell me when she's close enough to hear me whisper."

A moment later something brushed his nose.

"She's pretty damn close," Bob said.

"Yeah. Wearl, listen. As soon as we step into the hangar, I want you to watch the door. As soon as the first Shimmer crosses the threshold I'm going to drop him. Got it?"

"She does," Bob whispered.

Kalan took a deep breath. They were almost there. Almost to freedom, but this last step was going to be the most difficult. So far it had all been bluster and bravado, but now it would require real combat.

And the thing about real fights was that they were impossible to predict. Being right didn't mean you were going to win.

He approached the narrow doorway that led to the

hangar, his arm still tight around Sslake's neck. Through the entry he caught his first glimpse of one of the Nim-class fighters and a wave of nostalgia rolled over him.

Once upon a time these ugly long-nosed vessels had been his oasis. When he was piloting one of these babies, even though it was in defense of his captors, he hadn't felt like a prisoner. He'd felt free.

"Okay, here we go," he muttered, and he maneuvered Sslake through the door into the hangar.

As soon as they crossed the threshold Bob spoke, panic in his voice.

"Um, the Shimmers are yelling, telling us to release Minister Sslake. They've kept up their end of the deal, and they expect us to do the same."

"Wearl, where we at?" Kalan muttered.

Bob listened for a moment. "Wearl says now!"

Kalan released Sslake just as the guards had demanded, but then he levelled his pistol at the entryway and fired. He couldn't see his enemy, but according to Wearl they were standing there. He'd have to trust her.

He squeezed the trigger, firing round after round through the open doorway. He couldn't see if he was hitting anything or not, but he wasn't about to stop firing.

"Stop!" Bob yelled. "Wearl says to stop and take cover."

Kalan hesitated, but only for a moment. He had to trust his teammates—there was no other choice if he was going to get through this. He lowered his weapon and ran for a nearby stack of crates. If he could reach them, they would provide the ideal cover.

A strange boom split the air. Kalan had heard it before, but only rarely. It was the sound of the Shimmers' weapons. He didn't know what material the weapons were composed of that made them as invisible to the human eye as their users, but he did know they were effective. When he was nine he'd seen a prisoner torn to shreds by those weapons.

Kalan reached the crates and crouched behind them, his pistol at the ready.

The strange, muted booming sounds continued in the passageway. He didn't understand why the Shimmers weren't moving into the hangar since they had every advantage here. Kalan was the only one on his side who was armed, and the Shimmers were invisible.

After a few moments the gunfire ceased, leaving only a low hum in Kalan's ears.

To his surprise, Bob spoke. "Guys? Wearl says it's over."

Kalan blinked hard, confused. "What's over? How can it be over?"

"Well, according to her, she grabbed a gun from the one you shot in the doorway and mowed down the rest of them."

"Holy shit," Kalan said. "Seriously?"

Bob was silent for a moment. "Wearl, I didn't mean anything by 'according to her.' It's a turn of phrase, or whatever. I mean, thanks for saving our lives and all, but you don't have to be so sensitive."

Kalan stood up from behind the crates, marveling that they'd made it so far, but there was no time to dwell on it. They had to get going. He gestured to the two dozen Nim fighters parked in the hangar. "Minister Sslake, care to select our ride?"

The minister smiled. "I guess you owe me that much,

since you punched me in the face. That one." He pointed to the ship directly in front of him.

Kalan eyed the call number on the tail. "Ah, Nim 47. A solid choice." In reality the ships were identical, but there was no need to go into that now. "Wearl, it's going to take me a minute to prep the ship. Would you take out any Shimmers who try to get through that door?"

"She says she will," Bob reported.

"Good." Kalan imagined it wouldn't be long before the guards arrived in full force.

Bob cast a wary eye toward the ship. "Are all of us going to fit on that thing?"

Kalan opened Nim 47's hatch and pulled down the ladder. "They're designed to seat four. A pilot, a gunner, and a navigator. They are also forced to take a Shimmer along to babysit."

"Gunner," Bob muttered. "That sounds promising."

Kalan nodded. "It has railguns, sort of."

With that, he climbed aboard.

"Sort of?" Bob called after him. "What's he mean by that?" he asked no one in particular.

Kalan maneuvered to the cockpit and reached under the seat, his hand immediately settling on a small plastic box. The survival kit.

He hurriedly pulled it out and set it on the seat, then flipped it open and pulled out the knife.

Back when he'd flown for SEDE, they'd been strictly prohibited from touching the survival kit and checked when they exited the vessel to make sure they hadn't taken the knife or anything else from the ship.

But no one was watching him now.

Outside the ship, a Shimmer gun blasted a series of shots off.

"Everything all right?" he called.

"Yeah," Bob answered. "Three guards showed up, but our girl took care of them."

"Thank fortune for that Shimmer," he called as he touched the control panel and initiated the startup sequence.

He touched his right palm, searching for the hard spot. When he'd found it, he took a deep breath and pressed the tip of the knife into the flesh of his hand.

The Shimmers had proven they could track him via the chip. He had no idea if it could track him *outside* SEDE, but he wasn't going to take the chance. He gritted his teeth and kept cutting until he was able to pull the chip loose.

Then he grabbed a bandage from the survival kit and did his best to stop the bleeding.

"Okay, everybody but Wearl get up here," Kalan yelled. "Wearl, we need you to cover the door for another minute."

He then slid under the console and checked the weapons array, confirming the design was still the same as it had been back when he'd flown these ships.

Bob and Minister Sslake climbed aboard and settled into their seats, Bob taking the co-pilot's chair. Both of them eyed Kalan's bandaged hand as he emerged from under the console.

Sslake held out his hand. "I guess you'd better hand me that knife. I've got a chip too."

Kalan nodded and wordlessly handed over the blade.

The minister immediately went to work, stifling his grunts of pain as he removed the chip.

Kalan glanced at the console and saw that the startup sequence was complete. He hurried to the hatch and tossed out both bloody chips. "Wearl, let's go! Time to head out."

A moment later he felt something brush past him.

"Welcome aboard," he said with a grin. Then he pulled the door shut and latched it, creating an airtight seal.

"So we're ready then?" Sslake asked.

Kalan nodded. "Bob, slide under that console for me."

To his credit, the human did so without question.

"You see that green circuit?" Kalan asked. "When I tell you, pull it out of its slot."

Bob nodded. "Not a problem. Gonna tell me why?"

Kalan grabbed the controls and began taxiing toward the hangar door as he spoke. "These things were designed to be flown by prisoners in defense of SEDE, so they built in a failsafe. If this ship gets too far away from SEDE, the proximity meter knows it and it engages a kill-switch. Cuts power to the whole damn ship."

Sslake leaned forward in his seat. "That sounds like it's going to be a problem."

"It would, but I figured out a workaround. I was never able to use it, though, because I always had a Shimmer guard on board. Plus, the workaround has a nasty side effect."

"What's that?" Bob asked warily.

"The proximity meter is hardwired into the weapons array. To disable it I have to remove the whole damn thing."

"Wait. That means we can't use the railguns."

"Exactly." He punched a code into the console and the door at the end of the hangar slid open, exposing a massive airlock. Then he maneuvered the ship around so it faced the other ships. "I want to do one thing first, though."

He sprayed the other Nim fighters with a relentless barrage of ammunition.

After a few long moments he was satisfied. He may not have disabled every ship, but it would take them a while to figure out which ones were still operational. That should give them enough time to get clear.

As they taxied toward the airlock Bob said, "Geez, you're lucky you didn't put a hole in the prison."

Kalan chuckled. "Nah. Our railguns are nice, but SEDE is a tough old bird. I doubt we *could* breach her hull. Pull that green circuit, would you?"

Bob did as asked.

Kalan brought them to a stop inside the airlock and punched another code into his display. The door to the hangar closed and sealed, and the one to space beyond the ship opened.

Kalan touched the controls and a moment later they were cruising away from SEDE.

He turned to his shipmates and smiled. "That, my friends, is how you break out of a prison."

## 23

**Planet Tol: Outlands**

The fighter had taken them far enough, Valerie reasoned. Nothing but desert stretched before them, and they had lost sight of the city long ago.

"On the count of three," Valerie shouted as Garcia prepared to angle the fighter up. He hadn't figured out if there was an automatic pilot feature on this alien craft, so their best bet was to set it on a straight and slightly upward trajectory, then leap before it got too high.

"Three!" she shouted, and they all leaped, rolling across the sand.

It hurt, but they would heal.

*The story of her life.*

As they recovered they watched the fighter disappear, and then Valerie told them to hurry so they ran back toward the stashed *Grandeur*. With all this desert around and the measures they had taken to conceal it, they didn't expect the enemy would have found the ship.

As they were cresting a sand dune, Robin grabbed Valerie and Flynn and hissed for Garcia to get down.

"What is it?" he asked, taking a knee and glancing around.

"Five fighters, that way," Robin replied, pointing back the way they had come.

Garcia edged toward the peak, risking a subtle glance over. "They're pursuing the one we sent off, so that plan worked."

"At least one plan—" Robin started, but Valerie cut her off with a glare.

"No more of that," Valerie demanded. "It's over. What they were doing...it's barbaric. Humans aren't any better, I know that firsthand, but when a human does it? At least now in North America, or whatever they're calling it these days, we have systems in place to stop those kinds of crazies. These people need to be stopped too."

"I thought we came here to collect intel?" Flynn asked.

"And we will," Garcia said. "No more deviating from the plan. Right, Val?"

"You two clearly don't know her like I do," Robin said, shaking her head.

"From what I hear, no," Garcia replied, earning a glare from Robin and a simple clenched-jaw stare from Valerie.

"What I meant was, once Valerie sees injustice like this —people being treated unfairly, the innocent being hurt, whatever—she doesn't let it go. She'll do whatever it takes to see this end, if I'm right about her."

"Her? Really?" Valerie motioned and they started moving again, slower though, cautious of letting themselves be seen by the pursuing fighters. "I'm right here. You don't need to speak about me like I'm on some other planet. And why would we let it stand?"

"Because it's not our job?" Flynn replied. "Because it would probably be impossible to make a difference here? But not only that, what does it mean for the rest of the universe? Do you have any idea how many problem areas there are? How many planets have injustice going on as we speak? You won't live long enough to *see* them all, let alone fix them."

"Didn't you hear?" she replied, careful not to stumble over a ridge in the sand. "Vampires live a damn long time."

He rolled his eyes. "You're not really a vampire. Now that we're upgraded too, you're basically just a more badass version of me and Garcia here."

"One with fangs and red glowing eyes, thank you very much." She glanced back and figured they were probably in the clear, so they picked up the pace.

When they reached the *Grandeur* they climbed aboard, and Garcia immediately activated her defensive mode in case there were problems. It would, he said, scan for nearby fighter planes or worse, and immediately sound the alarm.

Valerie went straight to her spare armor, which was black with lines of red. Not completely inconspicuous, but very badass. Next she strapped on her sword and a pistol, and checked on the others.

"To be clear," Flynn said as he tried on his helmet and then slapped down the faceplate so that his voice sounded through the helmet's speakers, "are we effectively declaring war on behalf of the Etheric Federation?"

"No, of course not," Valerie said. "We don't work for the Federation, remember? As far as they know, anyway…"

"But we're strapping on our weapons, charging in, and killing their leadership?"

She pursed her lips, considering his words. "My plan is to take on their champion and whatever else they throw at us until the leader—this 'Bandian' character—reveals himself, if for no other reason than curiosity. Then yes, we take him out."

"Sounds like war," Flynn replied.

"He might be right," Garcia chimed in. "If nothing else, we should be honest with ourselves. We—I hate to say it— might want to call in, check with the colonel on this."

She shook her head. "We act first, ask forgiveness later."

"You sound like a Marine," Garcia replied with a laugh. "So the real question is, do we wait until tomorrow?"

"No way. I said that to keep them off-guard." She tossed everyone blankets and put one over her head like a robe. "We get into the city, find out what we can about setting up the revolution, and then when we show up for the fight tomorrow, everyone's primed. The revolution begins, or we find out it was a bunch of hooey. At least then we know."

The others confirmed the plan, and Valerie smiled broadly. "I love you guys, you know that?"

Garcia chuckled and nudged Flynn with his elbow. "Don't worry, she's just like that. The thrill of the fight gets her all emotional."

"Fuck you, Garcia. I'm just happy to have a team that's willing to one-eighty with me like that. We change plans and all of you are there with me, ready to throw away everything we have for the chance at helping these people."

"Everything we have?" Flynn asked.

"Well, yeah. Maybe our lives even, right? But on the other side of that spectrum, Bad Company might kick us out after this."

"You're one of Michael's favorites," Garcia countered. "Would they do that to you?"

"I guess we'll find out," she replied and headed for the door, where she paused.

"No," Garcia said flatly, eyebrow raised. "It's one thing to sneak back in there, another to bring the *Grandeur* with us."

"Unless the plan was to distract more of them and lead them on a wild chase so that they aren't looking as closely for us on the ground."

He sighed, then glanced at Flynn. "Can you fly?"

Flynn nodded.

"Good. Flynn will take to the skies while the three of us work our magic on the ground."

"Super-fun," Robin said sarcastically and sat back, waiting.

Flynn started the ship and got her airborne, and they were soon approaching the city. As they flew, Valerie sent a message to Kalan in case he was able to receive it, telling him to hurry back, it was time. Valerie pointed out a good place to disembark, and then they were out and *Grandeur* kept flying toward their destination.

Valerie watched her go, then saw the other fighters appear over the buildings and head straight for the ship.

"Good luck," she told Flynn as she led the other two into the city, keeping low with their makeshift cloaks on to avoid too much attention.

They were going to need it.

## 24

**Nim 47**

Kalan checked the monitor one more time, assuring himself they weren't being followed. The only ship it was registering was SEDE in the distance. The big ship was faster than their zippy little Nim, but it was far less nimble. With the hour's worth of space he'd already managed to put between them, there was no way SEDE would catch them now.

SEDE was farther from Tol than it had been yesterday when they had arrived, but not by too much. Kalan figured they were flying close to the planet during the Damu Michezo so they could make profitable runs to supply more fighters as needed.

For the first time since they'd escaped, Kalan allowed himself to relax a little.

Behind him, Sslake chuckled.

"Something funny, Minister?"

"I was thinking how strange it is that they named this class of ship 'Nim.'"

"Why's that funny?" Kalan asked.

"Nims are fat annoying insects on Tol. They hover around animals, feeding on the smaller insects the beasts attract."

"Ha," Kalan said. "I guess that makes sense. That was the function the Nims served for SEDE, too."

"How exactly does a prisoner become a pilot?"

Kalan shrugged. "About ten years back, some ships attacked SEDE and attempted to break out a group of terrorists. They failed, but suddenly everyone got real paranoid about defending the prison so they bought the Nims. Turns out Shimmers are really shitty pilots." He glanced over his shoulder at an apparently empty seat. "No offense, Wearl."

"None taken," Bob reported.

"Anyway, that was when they installed the kill-switches and recruited prisoners to fly the Nims. There was no shortage of volunteers, as you might imagine. I later found out I almost didn't make the cut. Lucky for me, the Yollin who was ahead of me on the list overslept the first day and was late for the informational lunch. The Skulla officials in charge of the program got pissed, and I got a spot on the roster."

"Huh," Minister Sslake said. "I still find it strange that they'd let prisoners pilot railgun-equipped ships, even with the kill-switch and a guard aboard. As you proved in the hangar, you don't have to be far from SEDE to do serious damage"

Kalan nodded slowly. "Yeah, that's true. At the same

time, that's why they were so selective. They only chose sabies, not those who'd been incarcerated for a crime. And the hangar was closely supervised when prisoners were present. Could someone have shot up the hangar like I just did? Maybe, but they'd have gotten a quick death for their efforts."

"If I'm able to win my position back from Warlord Nobir, there are going to be some serious reforms in that prison."

"Good," Kalan said. "Hey, I noticed you always call him 'Warlord Nobir' instead of 'the Bandian.' Why is that?"

Sslake answered with no hesitation. "Because he doesn't deserve the name. Do you know the legend of the Bandians?"

"Some race of great warriors, right? Extinct now."

"Yes," Sslake confirmed. "They were great warriors, but they were more than that. The stories say they were the first to unite the Vurugu system. Under their guidance, the Skulla and the Pallicons worked together for the first time. The three races united to defend the system from outside invaders. The Bandians were a uniting force,—basically the opposite of Nobir."

"So what happened to them?"

"No one knows. Sadly, that fact, along with so much else about them, has been lost to history."

The monitor chirped and Kalan prepared to enter Tol's atmosphere.

"This is it, Minister. You're almost home. How's it feel?"

"It feels good," the Minister said. "At the same time, it feels like we still have a lot of work ahead of us."

## 25

**Planet Tol: the Fighting Arena**

Their first stop was the bar where Robin had fought the twins. Not to cause trouble, but to look for two specific Skulla—the brother and sister they had met that night.

Working their way through the crowds of people, they were glad to see other aliens out and about. The whole city was alive with excitement, many of them glancing the humans' way as they went.

"Quickly," Valerie said. "One of these people will connect us and call the authorities."

"Maybe," Robin countered.

"What do you mean?"

"Look at their eyes," the woman replied. "That's not hostility, that's hope."

Valerie glanced around, then looked at Garcia, who nodded.

"They're glad someone challenged the system."

"Precisely," a voice said, and they turned to see the sister in the alley behind them with at least a dozen other Skulla in back of her. "If you're serious about challenging the system, we're with you."

Valerie nodded, looking at them all. "We can do this, but it has to be all the way. I've taken out leaders before, so I know the consequences. You'll need a system to replace the old one or chaos will ensue. You'll have to be ready to stand up against outside threats, allies of the old regime that might come for revenge. Do you understand?"

The Skulla nodded and the others murmured excitedly.

"How do you know about this, Wandrei?" It was the brother.

"I wasn't born yesterday," Valerie replied. "I was raised by a military group and trained to kill, but refused to follow their ways. When I broke free to put a stop to it in a place known as Old Manhattan, I found it was ruled by a group of evil men who were oppressing and killing my people. We threw them out, but that wasn't the end of our challenges."

"And what happened to it? The people?"

Valerie stepped up on a ledge where she could be better seen by those in the back, the moment very reminiscent of a day back on Earth when she had first started this whole leadership thing.

"I left that city, that world, only because I knew it was in good hands. To you I'll make the same promise. None of this will happen without your trust in me, so I'll tell you right now that I will not leave until you feel secure in my doing so."

Garcia leaped up join her, whispering in her ear, "The colonel might want a say in this."

She simply smiled. "Am I not Michael's Justice Enforcer? I refuse to believe that title was stripped from me the moment I left Earth, and if he or Bethany Anne were here, they would insist on this course of action—I'm certain of it."

He shrugged, putting up his hands in surrender. "Probably so."

"Given what I've said," Valerie turned back to the crowd, "are you still with me?"

Cheers rose from most of the crowd, though arena guards were inching their way forward.

"They're waiting for you," one of them announced, loud enough to be heard over everyone else.

"Excuse me?" Valerie asked.

"The arena awaits," the male continued.

Valerie turned to the brother and sister with a confused lift of her eyebrow.

"They can't be challenged like that and have it end it any other way," the sister explained.

"We were sent, many of us, to search the city." The guard added, "To let you know they are ready. Shall we let them know you're on your way?"

Certain it was a trap, Valerie nodded. "We'll head on over."

She held a finger to her earpiece and told Flynn to stand by, asking if he'd heard from Kalan yet.

"Negative," he replied.

"Keep on it, and be ready to swoop down if the situation gets out of control."

"Roger that."

She turned to her group and nodded as they threw off the robes. "Looks like we got dressed up for nothing."

"How about we see how crazy this gets, then decide," Robin replied. "The armor? Probably a good call."

"Listen," Garcia said as they started walking, the crowd leading the way like a parade. "I know you're throwing protocol to the wind and all, but I want you to remember that you're not alone out there. Valerie's Elites, right? We'll watch your back as long as you keep us in the loop."

"Valerie's Elites," she replied with a grin. "Of course, of course." She noticed a look go from Robin to Garcia. "What was that?"

Robin rolled her eyes. "Just anticipating how fast you'll run off on your own this time."

"*Valerie's* Elites, need I remind you?" Valerie scoffed. "If I feel I can take care of something better on my own you'll have to trust me."

"And I'm saying that you sometimes let your temper—or your ego—get in the way of the right decision in that regard."

"If I was more into this military stuff, I'd slap you for insubordination."

Garcia laughed. "That's not exactly how it works."

"In my army it would," Valerie countered. "Now quit your worrying and join the festivities." She gestured to the excited Skulla.

"As long as you realize this is nuts," Robin replied.

"And tell the colonel that we had nothing to do with it when he's chewing into you."

"Got it," Valerie replied.

They turned a corner to see the arena ahead, and she

smiled and waved to the crowd as she moved ahead of them.

"Wish me luck, ladies and gentle-Skulla," she said, then took a step back and drew her sword. "I promise one hell of a show!"

They cheered again at that, and she took off at a run. Better to get this part over with, she figured. As much as she was putting on an excited upbeat face, she knew the risks. She knew the gravity of the situation, but also knew that when she saw injustice like this—a system so messed up that people would sacrifice themselves or others to get ahead—it had to be torn down.

Since nobody else was doing that, it would have to be her.

Guards stood ready at the arena, but none of them made a move toward her. Clearly the leaders were committed to making an example of her. How misguided they were!

Valerie walked through arches of marble that had woven patterns of colored metals on them. Two guards cleared the way at the gates, eyeing her cautiously as she passed. One of them stood in her way, eyes full of uncertainty. She thought she was going to have to take him down, but when she got close he gave an almost imperceptible nod and said, "Some of us are with you. Remember that."

She nodded in return and strode out onto the sands. Before she had been wearing the equivalent of pajamas, but now she looked like the justice enforcer she was. Fully decked out with armor, gun, and sword, she walked right in, smiled, and held out her hands as she addressed the leaders.

"I came back early."

The female stood and raised a hand. "This Wandrei requested a fight with a champion. Normally we would reject such a request, but you have seen her power. Now you will see her fall. You want a fight? A fight you shall have!"

As she brought her hand down, the crowd cheered and the far gate opened.

Valerie blinked, trying to ignore the fact that she hadn't been addressed at all—had effectively been ignored—but then she shrugged it off. She had bigger problems, quite literally. A large male was lumbering toward her. Perhaps he had once been a Skulla, but now he resembled several of them merged together. His muscles had muscles, and bone grew like spikes along his back and shoulders.

Intimidating, perhaps, but she wondered how much it would hurt when she cracked one of those protrusions. She was about to move in for the attack when she heard stomping from behind, and she spun to see two more of the monstrosities plowing toward her.

Apparently a fair fight wasn't necessary to impress the audience. *Fine.* Valerie wouldn't give them one.

She turned and drew her pistol, cutting through the farthest one with three shots to the head and two to the chest, then hit the next-closest in the legs as she charged it, distancing herself from the third in the process.

As this second one fell she plunged her sword into the flesh between shoulder and neck, and then pushed off, pulling the sword free.

The result was that two were dead, sprawling to form a barrier in front of the third. He kept coming, much to his detriment. His legs caught on the corpses and he fell forward, hands out to try and catch himself.

Valerie was fast. She leaped forward, bracing herself, and hacking down with her sword. The monster's face went slack as the sword cut through skull and brain, and when she stepped back, her gore-covered visage glared upward.

"Enough appetizers," she shouted. "Give me the main course!"

Cheers erupted, and were almost enough to distract Valerie from the slight vibration that ran through the ground. She leaped onto her latest kill, then ran along the corpse and sprang off to jump to the arena's second-story ledge just as the electricity hit the arena floor and sent the bodies into wild spasms.

"Looks like that would've hurt," a Skulla said, offering Valerie a hand to help her up.

"Thanks," Valerie said, but she pulled herself up in one smooth motion. She glanced to the left and saw her friends hidden among the audience. Robin tilted her head as if to ask, "Now?" but Valerie shook hers, then stood on the railing with her arms stretched out.

"Is that the best you can do?"

"Why not try me on?" a female voice demanded, and Valerie turned to see someone coming out of the elite side, an area adorned with flowing tapestries that depicted past fighters.

If she had to guess, that was where the former victors

sat. Something was familiar about this one, the way her skin seemed to ripple in the sunlight.

Then she realized that it wasn't rippling, it was changing. This former champion was not a Skulla, she was one of the Pallicons she had met on the transport ship—the ones who had tried to take it over.

As Valerie approached the shifter replicated her form, but with a messed-up face—swollen eyes, a busted-in skull, and teeth sticking out of her cheek.

"Just thought I'd give you an image of what you'll look like in a few seconds," the Pallicon taunted, then morphed back into herself and approached one of the weapons stands as it rose from the ground. She pulled out a bright red rifle and smiled. "Tell me, do vampires burn?"

Valerie moved in at an angle, beginning to circle around this shifter. She analyzed her to see what made her so special. Anyone who would come in against Valerie after seeing how she dealt with the three monstrosities must have a reason to be confident.

The female charged forward and then leaped left and then right, pouncing like a lion. In the air she started shooting. Pellets of some sort hit the ground around Valerie and exploded into flames, one burst nearly catching her as she dodged them.

Playing target-practice as the target wasn't her idea of a good time, so she decided to close the gap. With no hesitation Valerie darted in, sword in hand, and cleaved through the Pallicon. The sword hit, but then was pushed out.

Valerie pursed her lips, confused, as she watched the female heal in what could only be described as liquid metal reforming itself.

"What the fuck are you?" Valerie asked.

"Furious, for one," the female replied.

The vampire thrust again, fully expecting to fail but *pushing* fear in case it worked.

The effect was surprising. Instead of a simple frightened expression or urge to tell the truth, the female started screaming as the sword wound refused to heal. Blood seeped out, and it was clear this female wasn't used to seeing her own. Valerie stumbled back, amazed and horrified. Had she caused that? Was it possible the power the Dark Messiah, Michael, had given her worked in unique ways on different alien races?

Now the Pallicon was pissed. Pissed, and likely scared. She charged again and thrust the rifle forward and a laser bayonet shot out, extending long enough to nearly catch Valerie. The second slash hit her armor in a burst of smoke and light, but then Valerie *pushed* fear again, thrusting, swiping, and slicing her opponent.

More screams, more blood.

The female leaped onto Valerie as metallic claws emerged from her hand. Valerie's claws grew now too and the they went at each other as the claw strikes too were nullified by the Pallicon's ability to heal herself and Valerie's armor.

"This isn't getting us anywhere," Valerie said, "so…sorry it has to be this way."

She leaped back and *pushed* fear as strongly as she could, and at the same time she drew her pistol and went to town. The shots ripped her opponent apart.

The shifter's screams were piercing and the look in her eyes was gut-wrenching, as if the female were seeing hell itself in that moment. And then she was on her back, barely alive and groaning in pain.

Valerie had stepped forward, ready to end it, when a loud voice cried, "ENOUGH!"

She looked up at the male beside the female leader. He wore grand robes, his head was shaved, and there was a circle of the red metal and gems on his brow.

The Bandian. It had to be.

## Planet Tol: the Fighting Arena

For what seemed an eternity the Bandian glared down at Valerie, eyes full of hatred. When he opened his mouth, it certainly wasn't to congratulate her on her victory, nor to challenge her to a fight.

Instead he shouted, "*KILL HER!*"

The crowds erupted in anger as guards streamed in and drones appeared over their heads, and everyone tensed for what was to come.

Suddenly shots started tearing into the guards from the audience and Valerie spun, searching for the source. Garcia was there with his rifle, but Robin wasn't visible at first until movement showed the drones moving for Garcia. Then, in a flash of black armor, Robin leaped through the sky, tearing through them with her short swords and then using one to take down the others.

A shot nearly hit Valerie and she was reminded that a whole army was moving on her. Warmth surged at the sight of her friends—Valerie's Elites—fighting at her side, in a sense. And that warmth intensified as she saw the Skulla rising, some of the fighters pushing their way out of the pits and attacking the guards, others moving down from the stands to join in.

Valerie had to keep the attention on her, so she ran straight for the Bandian. If his life was in danger, all firepower would be directed toward her.

Guards got in her way as she ran, but she cleaved through the first two, plowed through the next group by will and strength, and came out gun blazing. Drones formed a wall in front of the Bandian, and he leaped and landed on one of them.

"You think you know what we're capable of?" he shouted furiously. "You Wandrei always come to our home trying to tell us what we can and can't do, and you always leave in the end. One way or another, you're finished here."

He swooped down, kneeling on the drone like a miniature fighter as a small shield popped up and controls came into his hands. Other drones followed him, and they opened fire on Valerie.

One shot tore through her earlobe and another exploded on her body armor. She cursed herself for leaving her helmet on the *Grandeur*, but she would have to make do. Dodging back into the guards and using them as protection against the incoming drone shots, she returned fire before holstering her weapon and grabbing a guard with both hands. She heaved and sent him flying, his body hitting the drone and sending the Bandian off-course.

By the time the bastard had course-corrected, Valerie had pushed off one of the guards and taken her own drone.

She'd half expected it to have some fail-safe that wouldn't allow her to access the controls, but she brought the shield up and it responded, and now she and the Bandian were trying to shoot down each other's drone.

Since more drones were moving toward her, she saw that this wouldn't work for long. She also saw a welcome shape in the sky as the *Grandeur* appeared, her weapon systems ready. A battle was raging in the stands and on the arena's floor, so the best bet was for Flynn to focus on the drones.

"Welcome to the action," Valerie said into her comm, then dodged shots from the Bandian and swerved to avoid a drone that attempted a suicide mission against her.

"Lead them my way," Flynn replied. "I've got them covered."

She did just that, but as she crested the arena she saw that it wasn't going to be so easy.

"We've got company!" she shouted as she turned her drone back and flew for the *Grandeur*. A dozen fighter jets rose over the top of the arena, half of them laying down a barrage of fire against the *Grandeur* and the other half against the people below—bad and good alike.

Valerie needed to end this.

She spun her drone and found the Bandian, zooming toward him as shots narrowly missed her, and then she leaped.

His eyes went wide at her action, but there was nothing he could do. She was on him in an instant, claws digging into his flesh as she pulled him from the drone. She had him!

Except that as they fell, she saw the other leaders being

carried off by the drones to a larger ship behind the fighters. They weren't here to stop the battle; they were here to escort the leaders to safety.

And right before she and the Bandian hit the ground one of the drones grabbed him, snatching him away from Valerie and up into the sky.

She clawed at empty air and then slammed into the ground with a thud.

"Val!" Robin screamed, and she was there a moment later, shooting and slicing into the nearby enemy. Garcia provided covering fire, while above the *Grandeur* went into evasive maneuvers.

All the breath had been knocked out of Valerie, so she laid there for precious seconds as the chaos raged around her. Then Robin pulled her to her feet and they were running.

"They're escaping!" Flynn shouted over the comm. "What's the word, Val?"

She coughed up blood, glad she would heal soon, and said, "We'll meet you at the northeast side of the arena. At the top—get the ramp down and be ready."

"Sure, if I'm not shot down first!"

"You're not allowed to be," she replied with a grunt of pain. More shots plowed through the enemy and then Garcia was at their side, the three charging through the tunnels and up the stairs to the designated spot.

Valerie glanced at the fighting below. There was the fighter she had talked with, the one who had said she had been forced into the arena.

She saw Valerie and gave her a nod, then went back to slaughtering bad guys.

"Now!" Valerie called, gazing around for the *Grandeur*. "Where the hell are you?"

"Look alert!" Flynn called over the comm, dropping down nearly on top of them and pulling up at about the last minute. "They're on my tail, so go go *go!*"

All three jumped. Garcia barely made it, but Robin was there to pull him the rest of the way in.

Garcia shouted at Flynn to gun it and they were off, giving chase to the ship that had escaped with the leaders. She hoped her new friends could handle the riot at the arena, because following the Bandian was the only way to truly end this.

Valerie moved to her seat and assessed the situation. The screen showed four fighters on their asses and three more escorting the ship ahead, and then another dot. Something small was coming in fast.

And then a message came through. "What the hell have you sonsabitches gotten yourselves into?" Bob shouted. "Damn, looks like we arrived just in time to save your sorry asses."

"Woo!" Garcia shouted back. "I never thought I'd be saying this to you, but it's good to hear your voice!"

"Sit back and put on your safety belt," Valerie said. "These bastards mean business."

As she finished her sentence the three ships ahead maneuvered to intercept them, circling back with weapons firing while behind them the other fighters rose to attack Bob and Kalan.

Playtime was just getting started.

## 27

**Nim 47**

Kalan gripped the flight controls and banked hard to the right, flying toward the ships pursuing the *Grandeur*.

"Think we should tell them we have the rightful ruler of the Vurugu system aboard?" Bob asked.

"No!" Kalan and Sslake answered in unison.

"If they find out I'm aboard they might want us to land," Sslake pointed out, "and there's no way I'm missing this."

Kalan nodded. "Besides, we don't know if these communications are secure. The last thing we want is the Bandian finding out you're here."

"All righty," Bob sighed. "So we're going to fly into an air battle without any weapons?"

"The yanecat has already left the jungle on that one. Besides, *they* don't know we don't have weapons. Now hold onto something."

Kalan twisted the controls, sending them barrel-rolling east. He pulled out of it and let out a whoop of excitement as he positioned them directly behind one of the enemy fighters.

"Wearl says she's going to be sick," Bob said.

Kalan ignored the comment—he was too busy focusing on flying. He gunned it, racing straight toward the back of the enemy fighter.

As expected the fighter began evasive maneuvers, nose-diving to get out of Kalan's path.

Kalan pulled parallel to the *Grandeur*.

"Bob!" Valerie's voice barked through the comm. "What the hell? Why didn't you guys blow his ass up?"

Bob glanced at Kalan.

"Insecure communications," Kalan reminded him.

Bob rolled his eyes. "Uh, yeah, boss, that was a strate-gic...thing."

"Quit messing around!" Valerie ordered. "Shoot these guys out of the sky!"

Sslake leaned forward in his seat. "We need *her* to shoot them down."

Kalan nodded his agreement. "We'll try to maneuver them into a good position, but she needs to do the shoot-ing. Tell her that, but without telling her, you know?"

"Not really." He touched the button on the communica-tor. "Uh, boss, we're going to focus on moving the fighters into a good position. Then you can take the shot."

"What? Why?" Valerie asked.

"Uh, no reason. Seems like a practical way of doing battle. And I really can't say more than that, so please don't ask."

Kalan grimaced. "Artfully done."

"Really?"

"No. Hang on."

He raced forward, pulling ahead of the *Grandeur*, then banked hard left. The fighter on their tail followed suit, exposing the top of the craft to the *Grandeur*.

Valerie and company didn't waste the opportunity. Their weapons flashed, and fire erupted from the fighter's backside. It careened wildly toward the ground.

"Oh *hell* yeah!" Kalan shouted.

Bob tilted his head, listening to Wearl. "I'm not telling him *that*." He paused. "No, I don't want you to rip my fingers off, but I'm not saying—" He sighed and turned to Kalan. "Wearl says you're sexy when you fly."

"Right back at you, Wearl. You too, Bob." He angled the ship upward, trying to get above some of the other fighters. "Well, the good news is we're as fast as their ships, and I'm a better pilot than any of them."

"That's promising," Sslake allowed. "What's the bad news?"

Kalan checked his monitor and saw two fighters closing in on him. "Sooner or later they're going to figure out why we're not firing on them." He angled the Nim back downward, giving Valerie a clear shot at the two fighters without risking hitting him.

She took it, and another fighter spiraled toward the ground.

Sslake rubbed at his elongated chin. "We need a plan here. What are our options?"

Kalan hesitated. "There *is* one thing I've been contemplating, but it's risky."

"We're in a firefight without working weapons," Sslake pointed out. "Risky is where we currently live."

Kalan nodded. The minister was right, and risk was the predecessor of success, as the old Pallicon saying went. "Bob, I need you to slide under the console again."

The human paused. "Wait, what?"

"Do you think you could reconnect the weapons array?"

His eyes narrowed. "The one with the kill-switch in it?"

"That's the only one we've got."

"I think so." He thought a moment. "No, I *know* so. I can do it."

"Is that wise?" Sslake asked. "You said there's a proximity meter that shuts off all power if the ship gets too far from SEDE. I'm pretty sure this counts as 'too far.'"

"That's true," Kalan admitted, "but the thing is, I'm not exactly sure how it works. They had the device locked down so well I was never able to get a good look at it. Hold that thought a second."

A fighter dropped in behind them and Kalan threw them into another barrel-roll, narrowly avoiding a blast from the enemy fighter.

The *Grandeur* quickly repaid their attacker, shooting it down while it was still focused on Nim 47.

"You were saying?" Sslake asked.

"There are two options," Kalan continued. "It could be that the proximity meter tries to ping SEDE and if the pingback takes too long it activates the kill-switch."

Bob scratched his head. "In which case, if we hook up the weapons we lose power and fall like a dead bird."

"Yeah, but there's another possibility. It could be that SEDE pings our sensor. If they detect we're too far out, they send a signal to our proximity meter that activates the kill-switch. If that's the case, we're probably out of range."

"Probably?" Bob asked.

"I say we do it," Sslake immediately replied. "It's worth the risk."

Bob sighed for the umpteenth time. "Wearl agrees."

"Me too," Kalan said. "Sounds like we have a majority. Bob, do it."

The human unbuckled his harness and dropped to the deck. "If we die, someone tell Kalan's mom I regret never having made a move."

"If you had you'd be regretting a great many things," Kalan muttered. He touched the communicator and spoke into it. "Valerie, you there?"

"You know it," she answered. "We're doing our best to pick them off, but sooner or later one of them's going to get in a lucky shot."

"I know. Listen, I'm going to try to wedge myself between the fighters and the Bandian's ship. That way they won't be able to shoot at me without risking hitting their boss. And they'll be working hard to defend him, so that should give you the opportunity to take down a couple more."

There was a long pause. "Okay, do it."

"You'll avenge us if we die, right?" he asked.

"Most definitely, now get to work." She clicked off.

Kalan glanced down at Bob's legs, which were sticking out from under the console. "How we doing down there, buddy?"

"Not bad. Almost there. Trying to remember where this green circuit goes."

"It only fits in two slots. Put it in the one on the left." Kalan paused. "You sure you got this? If you mess it up you could fry the console."

"Don't worry about me; concentrate on flying."

Kalan had to admit that wasn't a bad idea. He climbed until he was a few hundred meters above the Bandian's impressive vessel.

"Hang on to something, Bob." he cautioned and pushed the controls in, causing the nose to drop. They dove toward the Bandian's ship.

Something clanged under the console and Bob shouted, "Ow! Son of a whore!" He paused a moment. "I'm trying, Wearl, but the way he's flying doesn't exactly lend itself to fine electrical work, you know?"

"Doing my best here!" Kalan responded, but he was only partially paying attention to the human's rantings. His eyes were fixed on the monitor—just as he'd hoped, the fighters had turned their focus on him when he dove at their leader's ship.

Now all he had to do was stay between the fighters and the lead ship so they couldn't get off a clean shot while also staying out of the *Grandeur's* way so Valerie could take out the rest of the fighters. Oh yeah, and also pray that the ship didn't drop dead when Bob finished reconnecting the weapons array.

"Almost got it!" Bob announced. "Now, when you say the left slot, you mean *your* left, correct?"

"What? No! Your left! Why would I tell you my left?"

"Okay, calm down."

One of the fighters maneuvered under them and Kalan realized almost too late that it was in the perfect position to take a shot at the Nim without endangering the Bandian's ship.

Thankfully Valerie had his back. The fighter exploded into a ball of fire before it managed to engage.

"Everybody ready?" Bob asked.

Kalan drew a deep breath. "Yeah. If the power dies, be ready to disconnect it immediately." He'd still need to run the startup sequence once the power came back online and the odds of him being able to do that before they crashed seemed very low.

But there was no need to mention that now.

"Okay, here we go."

There was a soft click as Bob slipped the circuit that powered the weapons array into place. It rang through the silent ship.

For a terrible moment, the power flickered. Every muscle in Kalan's body tensed as he prepared for the possibility of a crash-landing he knew none of them would survive.

Except maybe Wearl. He had no idea what her bizarre physiology was capable of withstanding.

"It's okay," Bob assured them. "Just a little power surge. We're up!"

Kalan blinked hard, still holding his breath. *Bob was right!* The weapons array monitor lit up as the weapons came online.

"Ha! Bob, you crazy bastard, you did it!" Kalan shouted.

The human slid out from under the console, a wide smile on his face. "You're damn right I did."

Kalan touched the comm. "Valerie, we're weapons-up. What do you say I take care of the last two fighters? I'll lure them away while you deal with the Bandian. What do you think?"

"I think you're jealous of all the fighters I got to blow up, but it sounds like a plan. I'm going to take that bastard down."

Kalan couldn't disagree with the first part of her statement. He *had* been a little jealous, but now he had his rail-guns. This was gonna be fun.

## 28

**Nim 47**

As another fighter crashed to the ground far below, Kalan checked his monitor. Only one enemy ship left, and that was the Bandian's.

The fighters had stuck fairly close to the Bandian's ship despite Kalan's best efforts to lure them away. They weren't going to abandon their boss—not with the *Grandeur* following so closely behind them—so Kalan had been forced to pick them off one by one.

He had to admit it was a rather enjoyable task. As the last of the fighters hit the ground he turned to his ship-mates. "How's it feel to share a ship with a true artist?"

"I don't know if killing should be considered an art," Sslake said, "but I have to admit that was some impressive flying."

Bob looked annoyed. "I was hoping I'd get to be the gunner."

"I'm a fan of multitasking."

"Wearl says to tell you you're even more sexy when you're cocky." He tilted his head, listening. "Okay, that's where I draw the line, Wearl. I am *not* saying that part! Do you kiss your invisible mama with that mouth?"

Through the cockpit window he saw Valerie doggedly pursuing the Bandian, firing relentlessly at his ship, but the warlord had a hell of a pilot. He was avoiding most of the shots, and the few that had hit didn't seem to have done any critical damage.

Minister Sslake put a hand in Kalan's shoulder. "Where are we?"

Kalan peered through the window at the ground. "I don't know. Over a jungle or something?"

"Coordinates, man! What are the coordinates?"

"Oh!" Kalan tapped the corner of the monitor that displayed their current location, pointing it out to the minister.

"Damn this dust-tongued jungle!" Sslake exclaimed. "I suspected as much."

Kalan and Bob exchanged a worried glance.

"Care to fill us in?" Bob asked.

"When Warlord Nobir was first coming to power, he lived in this jungle. Set up this whole big base of operations here. This was where I busted him the first time for his genetic experiments. There should be a mountain up ahead."

Kalan glanced out the window. "I see it."

"I'd bet another year in SEDE that's where he's headed."

"We better share that information, then." Kalan touched the communicator and told Valerie.

She listened to his rundown and asked, "You're sure about this? How do you know?"

Kalan touched the mute button. "Guess it's time to take our medicine." He clicked the comm back on. "We don't, but Minister Sslake is sitting right behind me and he's been here before. He busted Nobir in this jungle back in the day."

There was a long pause.

Finally, Valerie said, "Are you telling me Minister Sslake has been in your ship this whole damn time?"

"Yeah. I mean, you sent us to get him."

"I assumed you'd failed when you showed up and started dogfighting! I want him taken to safety. We'll handle the Bandian. You head back to the city, and we'll join you as soon as we're done here."

Kalan opened his mouth to argue, but Bob started speaking before he could.

"We copy you, Valerie. Be careful. We'll see you back at the spaceport." He clicked off and shook his head. "Never thought I'd see the day when *I'd* be the voice of reason."

Kalan looked at the human in disbelief. "You're kidding me right now. We're not really leaving, right?"

Bob shrugged. "I don't much want to, but she has a point. Sslake is the priority. Besides, I don't know how they do things here on Dust World, but where I come from an order's an order. Kinda takes the choice out of it." He paused for a moment, listening, then his face scrunched up in anger. "Well, same to you, Wearl! And twice on Sundays!"

It was clear the Bandian's ship was headed toward the

mountain, and Valerie followed closely behind. Kalan veered east, angling toward the city.

"Hold on," Sslake said, "there's something else. This isn't simply the Bandian's base of operations, it's where he trains his genetic warriors. He's got an army down there." He nodded toward the *Grandeur*. "I don't know how many soldiers she has on that ship of hers, but it can't be more than a hundred or so, right? That's not enough."

Bob's face drained of color. "Uh, it's decidedly less than that."

Kalan gripped the controls. "Where's he keep this army?"

"There're some outbuildings near the base of the mountain. He's probably already sounded the alarm, but it'll take a while for them to get up to his headquarters. That's our only advantage."

Kalan thought for a moment. On the one hand Valerie had given them a direct order, and a logical one at that. On the other, there was no way in sun-parched hell he was going to leave her and her small crew to face an army alone.

There wasn't even a decision to make, he realized.

He turned in his seat and looked at his shipmates. "Here's what we're going to do. We're going to make one pass over these outbuildings and the road to the mountain. Any troops we see headed up that way, we're going to light them up."

"But our orders!" Bob objected.

Kalan held up a hand. "After we make one pass I'm going to set us down and hand the ship over to you, Bob.

You'll follow orders and take Sslake to safety, and I'll do what I can on the ground for Valerie."

Bob shook his head. "Kalan, don't be an idiot. One male, even a Grayhewn, can't face an army. All you'll do is get yourself killed."

Kalan smiled weakly. "You may have a point there, but it's my decision to make. Besides, I won't be taking on a whole army. With any luck we'll take out most of them from the air."

"It is a noble gesture," Sslake said. "Your sacrifice won't be forgotten."

Kalan raised an eyebrow. "Um, just so you know, I'm planning to live through this thing."

Bob got that familiar look he wore when he was listening to the voice the rest of them couldn't hear. "Wearl says she's coming with you."

Kalan shook his head. "I appreciate the gesture, but it's not necessary."

"She says she'll gouge your eyes out if you try to stop her."

"Er, okay then." Truth was, having an invisible and possibly crazy ally on his side didn't sound too bad.

They flew on for a few minutes, circling the base of the mountain.

"There!" Sslake said, pointing at a small clearing in the jungle. Kalan squinted and was able to make out some buildings.

He dove toward it, and as he got closer he saw the road snaking up the mountain. When they were closer still he saw several large six-wheeled transport vehicles, some parked near the buildings and a few already making their way up the road.

"Okay, here we go," he muttered, then fired on the vehicles.

He started with the ones near the building, circling and raining down devastation with his railguns. Then he began working his way up the road.

When he'd reached the last vehicle he considered circling back for another pass, but the flashes of light from one of the remaining vehicles convinced him otherwise. It was firing back at him.

He couldn't risk Minister Sslake. He spotted a place where the road widened and set the ship down.

As he made his way toward the hatch Bob called, "Hey, Grayhewn! I'm glad Valerie stuck me with you."

Kalan smiled. "Me, too, now get the hell out of here. Wearl and I have an army to fight."

## 29

## Bandian Base

Valerie let out a whoop as the last of the enemy fighter planes from the mountain base exploded in the sky and rained debris down on the jungle below. She couldn't help but be amazed at the contrast of this jungle and the desert surrounding the city.

Whatever the Bandian was up to out here, she was certain that the Skulla and others back there would have turned on him long ago if they'd known he was keeping this a secret.

The Bandian's ship was out of sight, but a blip on the screen meant they didn't have to worry.

"She's touching down just past that mountain," Flynn said, pointing to a tree-covered mountain on the display.

"Bring us around gently in case it's a trap," Valerie commanded, "and let's be ready to move."

"What's the plan, boss?"

"Assuming we get in close enough?" She considered,

watching as Kalan's ship moved in for a sweep and wondering if he was following orders. "Land the ship at the base, then we move up—"

"Holy shit," Garcia declared as what was clearly the Bandian's base came into view.

He wasn't *hiding* here; it was more like his fallback defensive position. Built into the side of the mountain was a metallic structure that resembled an animal's head, similar to a panther's. Its turrets swiveled, and warnings flashed across the *Grandeur's* screen.

"Get us out of here!" Garcia shouted to Flynn, and they dove as rounds peppered the sky.

Valerie threw herself into her chair and took over. Her reflexes were faster than Flynn's, so she was their best bet.

"No," Flynn said, gesturing toward the base as they swerved. It was in their view one minute and gone the next. Skulla had now opened fire from the ramparts as well. "We need to get you in close, drop you off, and fly out of here before they know you're there."

"It's too risky for you," she argued, "and for the ship."

"At least you put me first," he replied with a laugh. "We'll land farther down the mountain and then double-time it up here to join the fight. Keep them occupied from the outside."

"That *was* fairly close to what I was going to say, minus you serving as a focus for their fire."

"You need to catch him," Garcia interjected, "meaning we can't afford delays. Who knows what he has going on in there?"

More dodging and shooting, and Valerie nodded—there

wasn't time for hesitation. "Bring her close, and Robin and I will jump."

"Always fun hanging out with you," Robin said with a wink. "At least I know it will never be boring."

"Nope, killing bad aliens who enslave populations and force others to fight for their enjoyment is not boring." Valerie laughed. "Hell, it seems there are enough of those bastards out there to keep us from being bored for a long time."

"You two want to keep chatting, or jump?" Garcia asked, having already opened the hatch so that wind was blowing through the ship and making it hard to hear.

"Stop talking," Valerie shouted back at him. "I'm getting ready to jump here."

He flashed a smile and tossed her and Robin their rifles, and turned back to help Flynn.

"Ready," Robin shouted.

"Go time!" Valerie replied, pulling on her helmet as Robin did the same. They both leaped.

As soon as they'd left the ship Valerie started to wonder if she'd made the wrong move here. Not that there was much time for that, as the ground was coming up fast. Trees and overgrowth blanketed the jungle floor, and for an instant she imagined it covered in silver spikes, waiting for her to make contact.

And then she was rolling through bushes and large leaves, a few branches cracking but no spikes—nothing to pierce her armor.

She ended her roll on one knee, eyes to the sky watching the *Grandeur*'s shields light up as she took a hit and then roll out of the way as a new barrage came at her.

As she disappeared Valerie saw Kalan's ship streak across the sky too.

It was just her and Robin now.

"You going to sit here finding shapes in the clouds," Robin asking, pulling her to her feet, "or help me take down this fortress?"

Valerie readied her rifle, quickly checked to ensure her sword was in place, and pointed to the clouds. "That one kinda looks like a pile of dead Bandian followers."

Robin glanced up and raised an eyebrow. "Huh. Looks like a cloud to me," she replied, then started running up the mountain.

"No fun," Valerie hissed as she ran after her, soon catching up so that they ascended side by side.

The fortress loomed ahead, but the shooting had stopped. The silence was interrupted by a Skulla shouting orders and the sound of metal grinding on metal.

As they grew closer it became clear that the Skulla were pulling back into the base. It was going into lockdown mode!

No talking now. Both women knew they needed to put all their energy into making it to that fortress before entry became impossible. They went into vampire mode, eyes glowing red and muscles throbbing with power. The broad jungle leaves fluttered as they flew past like the wind, and it wasn't until they were within a few paces of the base that the Skulla even noticed them.

Shouts of alarm filled the upper rampart. A team of Skulla fighters decked out in exoskeleton-enhanced body armor and carrying weapons almost as large as themselves came through the doors as more orders were yelled behind them.

A bright light shone from one of the weapons and a plasma blast tore through the ground directly behind Robin, but Valerie wasn't letting those things make contact. She leaped and pushed off a large tree, sending it to fall in one direction as she flew in the other toward the ledge with the warriors. She filled the first line of them with holes by firing on the way down.

More blasts came, one scorching through her body armor most of the way, and then she charged, slamming her sword into the neck of the closest modified Skulla. The armor resisted but her strength was too much for it. The armor gave with a crunch and her sword slid into the Skulla's neck.

She held the sword with one hand and propped her rifle on the Skulla's shoulder, using the dead creature as a shield against the remaining shooters as well as a prop.

A thud came from behind her and she stiffened, but then sensed Robin—even recognized her scent through the armor. Nothing to worry about from that direction, she realized as Robin opened fire at some other enemy. Valerie would focus forward, then see if her friend needed help.

With a kick she sent the corpse into the last two Skulla in her way, following it with a charge and then several shots to the face of one. The second dropped his weapon and tried to take her with two blades that emerged from the exoskeleton, but she deflected the first strike with her shoulder armor and the second with her sword before coming down with a pommel-strike that smashed the Skulla's faceplate.

As he backed up, terror on his face, he forgot to watch where he was going and plummeted right over the side. A thud sounded below, but that wasn't where Valerie's attention was.

Her eyes went wide at the sight of the doors, now closed nearly all the way with a group of Skulla right inside them—or something moving in the darkness anyway. A glance over her shoulder showed Robin sniping at another group that had left the safety of their base to come at them from behind.

"No time for that," Valerie shouted, pulling her friend along.

At first Robin resisted, but when she realized what was happening she accelerated and the two slid through the narrow gap, firing as they did so that the first line of Skulla defense fell.

A loud thump sounded, followed by another that made the room shake. It was dark, though their vampire eyes adjusted quickly enough.

Finally Valerie saw it—a Norrul like the ones she had fought on arrival in this system, only this one was twice as large as those she had faced. He had a line of other Norrul behind him and they were all in some sort of hangar bay where fighter ships were being built along the walls.

"We're not here to fight you," Valerie said, slinging her rifle over her shoulder and sheathing her sword. "I know you're sla—"

She was cut off as the Norrul let out a roar and charged. As he drew closer, it was apparent his rock-like carapace covered most of his body. It was thick and jagged, forming spikes on his arms and shoulders.

At the last minute he rolled, coming up with a spiked attack then switching to a leg-sweep that was much too fast for his size. Robin leaped toward him, but one of his arms hit her and slammed her into the floor. She skidded across it as more Norrul charged toward her.

This was getting out of hand. Valerie went for her sword again, but the Norrul grabbed her arm and smashed it into the ground. The impact sent a shock through her— the armor had cracked! *Damn* this dude was strong.

But she had learned something in her first encounter, so she knew that the Norrul weren't their enemy.

She hit him with two strong elbows to the sides of the head, just enough to distract him so she could scoot out from beneath him and get some distance. More Norrul were closing on her, and out of the corner of her eye she saw Robin taking on several.

"We're not here to fight you!" Valerie shouted. "The Skulla have turned against the elites. They've risen for freedom, and you can have it too!"

There was a definite change in attitude in parts of the room, but not from all the Norruls equally. The large one didn't seem to care. That, or his blood-rage had taken over and he was beyond the point of comprehension.

When he charged again, she dodged left and came around with a kick to his back that sent him sprawling. He was up before she knew it, however, throwing wild punches her way.

"Aren't you listening?" she shouted, slamming him in the side of the head. "We aren't your enemy!"

One of his punches connected with her chest and sent her stumbling backwards, but the next she blocked with her forearms before ducking and butting her head into his nose.

This sent him staggering back into a couple of his own, who turned on him. He was too much for them, though, and quickly had them on the ground.

Another ran for Valerie and she prepared to attack, but he held up his hands and said, "No, no! He's with *them*. He's with the Bandian!"

Valerie shoved this one aside as the first Norrul attacked again and went at him with a series of quick strikes—knee, knee, elbow, uppercut, sweep to the leg. The large Norrul fell with a thud that shook the room.

"Is this true?" She pounced on him. "Are you with them, or us? Declare yourself now!"

"Die," he grumbled, reaching for her throat.

Deflecting the blow, she decided this was over—she grabbed his rock carapace in two spots and used all her strength to pull it apart. It splintered and then with a massive *crack* the rock came off, leaving behind green tendrils of ooze and a Norrul who screamed like a tortured pig.

Valerie pulled her sword and raised it high, saying, "You already had your last chance, but hell...I'm a sucker for having more than one life. Change of heart?"

Through the pain he managed to glare at her with wild eyes and grunt through clenched teeth, "Eat rock and die as you shit."

She didn't have the slightest idea how to take that insult, but it didn't sound pleasant. With a sigh she thrust the sword into his chest where the rock had been removed and turned it.

A low grunt and he was gone.

Instinct pulled her back, sword dripping but held at the ready. The rest of the Norrul had taken a step backward and now they knelt, heads bowed.

"What's this?" she asked, glancing at them as she lowered her sword.

One of them cautiously lifted his eyes to meet hers and said, "We are in your debt. He was the Bandian's person, the one over us. You have set us free."

"Then go back to your homes, your loved ones, your—"

He held up a hand, cutting her off. "No, we will not. It would be a disgrace not to pay you back. You said you're here to take down the Bandian? Then we are with you."

A glance at Robin showed she was on board, so Valerie shrugged and said, "Welcome to the team. Care to point me in the right direction as a start?"

The Norrul who had spoken stood and smiled as the room filled with the clanking of the rest getting to their feet.

"Follow me," he said, and led the way.

So she did, unslinging her rifle and holding it at the ready, glad to have this wall of rock people preceding her in this dark fortress.

## 30

**Planet Tol: the Jungles**

Kalan's eyes scanned their surroundings as he trotted up the hard-packed dirt road.

He'd set them down a bit up the mountain from where they'd seen the transport vehicles, which meant any of the genetically-modified warriors going up to assist their warlord would have to pass this point.

But he'd also set them down in a wide section of the road. Two versus an unknown number of warriors was bad enough, but facing them on a wide stretch would be a disaster.

"You with me, Wearl?" Kalan asked as he jogged. Something brushed up against his arm. "I'm going to take that as a yes. We need to find a narrow place—something we can actually defend."

They trotted onward in silence for a few more minutes. The road was rising steeply now, and up ahead he saw a cliff overlooking a narrow section of road. If they could make it up there, it could be an ideal spot.

"I know what you're thinking, Wearl. How are two people going to defend this road from an army, even if those two people are as smart and good looking as us? That's an excellent question. My hope is that in the chaos after we shot up their little caravan they'll be disorganized and panicked and trickle up the road in small groups rather than in an organized assault."

They reached the cliff, and Kalan stared up at it for a moment. It was only about twenty feet high, but it would give them a nice position to work from.

"This could work, Wearl. This could work very well. Here's hoping Shimmers can climb."

He found a trail that looped around behind the cliff, and it took them less than five minutes to make it to the top. Then they waited.

A few minutes later the first soldiers came up the road. As Kalan had hoped, it was a small group. There were only five of them, and they were on foot.

They were taller than the average Skulla, probably a little over five feet. They were also lean and fast. Clearly these genetic alterations were much more practical than Zoras' and some of the other strangely-shaped Skulla Kalan had seen over the years.

"Here we go," Kalan whispered. He had the sudden wild notion that maybe Wearl wasn't here at all. Maybe she was back down the road, or even still on the Nim 47.

If she *wasn't* here, he was in some serious trouble. Granted, he had a solid position, but he was armed only with Bob's pistol and the knife from the survival kit on the Nim—not exactly an ideal sniper-weapon set.

But no, he'd felt her brush against him. He had to trust her.

"Wait until they're about ten yards out," Kalan whispered. "Then we—"

The strange boom of the Shimmer weapon firing cut him off before he could finish. The five men fell in six shots.

"Okay, that works too." Kalan grinned. "Wearl, I'm pretty glad you decided to tag along."

They watched until three more soldiers appeared. Again Wearl dropped them efficiently, but this time it was from a solid fifty yards.

Kalan bit his lip, considering too late whether she should have waited until they got closer. The next Skulla who came down the road would see those bodies and be on high alert or decide to get organized.

Just as he'd feared, the next group of troops—six of them this time—paused seventy yards away, then turned back.

Kalan cursed softly. He wasn't foolish enough to think they'd left for good.

"We need to be ready, Wearl. The rest of this won't be as easy."

He saw smoke rising above the thick jungle in the distance, and a moment later he heard the unhealthy rumble of a damaged engine. Finally he saw the transport.

The vehicle had sustained heavy damage during their aerial attack, but it was still running and Kalan could only guess how many were hiding inside it behind the heavily-armored exterior.

As soon as the transport came into sight Wearl started firing again. She hit it with round after round, but still it kept coming. It was moving fast now, powering through Wearl's assault.

Kalan didn't even bother firing. If the vehicle could withstand Wearl's rifle, his sad little pistol didn't stand a chance.

The vehicle banged to a stop at the bottom of the cliff right below them. The cliff had a slight overhang, giving the vehicle a bit of cover.

"*Go!*" a Skulla in the vehicle yelled. "Get up there and rip them apart!"

A dozen soldiers poured out of the transport and started up trail that led up the cliff.

"Here we go," Kalan muttered.

They were positioned behind some rocks, which gave them nice cover from the trail behind them.

Now that the Skulla were close he could finally join in the fun. As Wearl's rifle boomed to his right, he took aim and fired on the troops rushing up the trail. Three of them fell quickly to his weapon, but they were coming faster than he could take them down.

Thankfully Wearl picked up his slack, dropping any Skulla Kalan didn't. A few moments later all twelve were down.

Kalan allowed himself to smile. "I gotta say, Wearl, I like having—"

Something grabbed his ankle, pulling him to the

ground. He cried out in surprise as his face slammed into the rocky soil.

Wearl's rifle boomed again, but a moment later he heard something clatter to the ground beneath the cliff.

He quickly rolled over and saw a huge Skulla grinning down at him. He was as tall as his companions had been, but much more muscular. Kalan figured he was part of a different genetic batch.

It took Kalan a moment to put together what had happened. They'd been so focused on the soldiers coming up the trail that they'd completely disregarded the cliff itself. It was nearly sheer so it had seemed unlikely that anyone would be able to climb it, but apparently that was what this huge Skulla had done.

He'd managed to bring down Kalan, and apparently he'd knocked Wearl off the cliff.

Now he glared down at him, his rifle trained on the Grayhewn's chest. "Tell your friend that being invisible is only effective if you don't have a loud-ass rifle announcing exactly where you are."

"Tell your friends I hope they're enjoying their time in hell." With that Kalan lashed out with his right foot, slamming it into the inside of the Skulla's knee.

The Skulla cried out in pain and stumbled to the side.

Kalan rolled to a crouch, then lunged at his attacker. Perhaps a bit too hard, he realized a moment later.

He slammed into the Skulla, carrying them both over the cliff.

Kalan's stomach lurched as they fell and the world spun around him. He only had time for one thought: he was really glad he was on top.

The big Skulla softened the landing, but it was still a hell of an impact. The air rushed out of Kalan's lungs and he gasped frantically as he rolled off the big male.

He was still trying to regain the breath that had been knocked out of him when, to his surprise, the Skulla started to struggle to his feet.

"You've gotta be kidding me," Kalan said between gasps. His hand went to his belt, searching for the pistol, but instead it found the knife.

He attacked first, punching the Skulla in the face with his empty hand. When the male stumbled backward, Kalan slashed his throat.

When he went down Kalan found his pistol and put a round in his chest, finishing the job.

He looked around frantically, searching for anyone, friend or foe. "Wearl, you here? Are you okay?"

There was no response.

He heard footsteps pounding as a lone soldier sprinted up the road toward him, but the familiar Shimmer rifle boomed and the Skulla fell.

Kalan smiled. "Wearl! You're alive!"

He wished he could grab her by the shoulder or give her a hug to show his happiness, but neither was practical with an invisible ally so he just smiled.

They waited a while longer, but no one else came up the road.

"What do you say we see if Valerie needs a hand?" he asked.

**Planet Tol: the Bandian's Base**

This base's tunnels seemed to go on and on, and wound up and down. Valerie had started to doubt these Norruls, wondering if they were leading her and Robin into a trap, but when the waves of modified Skulla had shown up and the Norruls had led the charge against them her doubts were replaced by awe and admiration.

Not only were the Norruls loyal, they were badasses.

If she were being honest with herself, that large Norrul she had killed had probably come the closest to scaring her in a long time. Having a whole team of them on her side was therefore very welcome.

They heard shooting in the distance, and at one point they came to deep windows that let them see outside. Below a turret exploded and then a figure dashed toward the base, followed closely by another as fresh rounds exploded the dirt behind them.

More shots rang out, and a Skulla fell dead.

"Keep moving," the Norrul said, motioning them on, but then he asked, "Friends?"

"Friends."

They kept going. The Norruls were murmuring among themselves and glancing her way.

"What is it?" she finally asked, made anxious by the lack of attacks for the last few minutes. She was also annoyed at the smell of this place as they entered what must've been the brain, if you thought of the base like a panther. It was somewhere between burnt metal and maple syrup, oddly enough.

"You're here. You made it this far," the Norrul replied. "Your friends are holding it down out there, and… You say the Skulla in the city have risen against the leaders, yes?"

She nodded. "That's correct."

"It's really happening then." He beamed, nudging the Norrul to his right. "I never gave up hope. This one… He lacks faith."

"Faith in what?" she asked.

"The tales of a great leader, one who will set us free and lead our people to a new way of life. To freedom."

Valerie frowned. It was a pretty typical legend for any group kept in slavery, but she didn't like the idea of anyone looking to her as the fulfillment of some prophesy or whatever this was. Apparently neither did the Bandian, because he chose that moment to show himself.

They had entered a room that was filled with wires, flickering boards, and robotic limbs. The Bandian sat at its center in a strange-looking metal chair surrounded by more metal and wires. Why anyone would choose this as a throne was beyond Valerie's comprehension, but hey–they *were* aliens, after all. Or rather, here *she* was the alien.

"You were free," the Bandian declared, "and I was that leader. I set you free from your lack of order, from your lack of purpose. Now look what you've accomplished, only to throw it all away."

The Norruls clearly detested the male and yet they knelt, heads bowed.

"I don't... What's happening?" Valerie asked.

"Ah, you don't know their ways yet then?" He shook his head, his expression annoyed as if he were about to explain something to a child. "I'm still their true master, so they can't turn against me. They will be punished for what they have done so far, but to go any farther would mean death."

"They aren't yours anymore," Valerie declared. "Surrender, or your life is forfeit."

"Do you always talk like that?" He laughed. "Shut up and fight me."

With that he waved his hand, and the mechanics of his throne folded around him but left an opening in front of his face shielded by glass so she could still see it. The room around them whirred, coming to life, and even as his throne became a giant mech other parts of the room got ready to attack, including mini-turrets, small drones, and more.

"Holy fucksticks," Valerie declared, taking a step back.

While the large Norrul had been intimidating, he had been nothing compared to this mech before her. It was even worse, because back on post-Great Collapse Earth mechanics were fairly limited. In her mind this was straight out of a story told late at night—something that couldn't possibly be real.

Yet here it stood, large cannon and missiles preparing to fire, metallic blade whirring like a chainsaw.

"*GET OUT OF HERE!*" she shouted to the Norruls as she ran for the mech. As far as she could figure, it would have a limited range of motion within the room. It was large, and slower than her.

Robin had already made a move, but toward the mini turrets around the room—just as they opened fire.

She took out one and shouted, "I'll get these, you get him!"

"Agreed!" Valerie shot back, already moving for the mech but circling, trying to figure out the best method of attack. It swung its massive metal arms, coming in for her with that whirring blade but instead carving a line in the floor when she dodged.

If the Bandian had this, what else was out there on this planet and in the rest of the universe? Valerie felt like her mind was going to explode just thinking about it so instead she focused on the fight, diving out of the way as a barrage of little missiles tore into the wall where she had been. They exploded, opening the room into a chamber that led into the mountain behind it.

Matching the mech with firepower wasn't possible, so she would have to be smart here.

When the cannon lifted and prepared to fire she threw herself into the new chamber and rolled, and the blast exposed another chamber.

"Watch it!" a voice shouted, and she spun to see Kalan.

He was a sight for sore eyes, but right now wasn't the best time for catching up.

"Trouble—" she started as the mech came tearing through the remaining wall into this chamber. The Bandian's face lit up with excitement.

"Two for one deal," he said with a laugh, and pounded the room with rounds.

*Boom!* Boom-boom-*BOOM!*

"You forgot me," Robin declared, sliding under his legs and blasting up at the glass as she did.

No good.

She recovered, scrambling to get out of the way as the mech's foot tore into the floor where she had been, and caught up with Valerie.

"We got a plan for this thing?" she wondered.

"Yes—fucking tear it up."

Valerie charged as booming shots came from Kalan's direction, and she fired as Robin shot from where she stood. Nothing worked, however, and the mech continued its rampage, tearing more walls apart.

"Try its back!" a Norrul shouted, and she turned to see that they were still there and still kneeling.

"Get up and fight!" she shouted. "What're you doing?"

"You heard him, he—"

Valerie dove as a barrage of missiles went off nearby, then fired some more. Fine—if the Norruls weren't going to help physically, she could at least try out their advice.

She ran for the mech and leaped, but didn't quite make it. A moment later the Norrul knelt at her side and said, "Here."

It took her a moment to process his offer, but then she

leaped onto and off his back, and was on the mech. She grabbed a protrusion with one hand, pulling herself up the back and onto the top, and she jammed her sword into the point with the most wires.

Smoke bellowed, sparks flew, and a mech arm came toward her. She used it to her advantage, swinging off the limb and onto the front of the mech, where she commenced with slamming her elbow into the glass over and over.

It was too thick, but that didn't mean she'd give up. As the mech reached for her again she held tight, grabbing the arm and using *it* to bash the glass. Its blade whirred, and the glass splintered. The mech was thrashing, weapons going off in every direction and exploding against walls, even hitting other tech that then exploded.

The glass hadn't given completely, but now it was weak. Valerie slammed her armored hand through it, grabbed the Bandian by the throat, and yanked. She pulled out his throat and turned to get off, but froze. Out of the corner of her eye she had seen a change, and when she looked back she realized that this wasn't the Bandian at all. It was one of those damn shapeshifters she had first encountered when they'd tried to hijack Kalan's transport ship.

If this was a shifter, where was the Bandian? The mech fell and Valerie leaped for cover as a new barrage of explosives hit the building.

Robin appeared with Kalan at her side, both looking frantic.

"It wasn't the Bandian," Valerie explained. "He's still out there, and means to take the whole place down on us."

"RUN!" Robin and Kalan shouted in unison, and they

all took off for the nearest hole, the Norruls following closely behind. The ceiling was caving in and flames licked the walls, and as the group burst out of the chamber they realized they were in trouble. A line of modified Skulla, a couple of mechs, and several large Norruls were lined up for the fight.

"Well, fuck." Valerie turned to Robin and took her hand, giving it a squeeze. "Die trying, right?"

"Damn straight!"

They drew their weapons and charged, shouting their war cries at the top of their lungs as the enemy assault began.

Only the bullets didn't hit, because the Norruls on the enemy side had rolled forward and now formed a barricade against the attackers. The Norruls behind her were joining in, and the one from earlier came up beside Valerie and Robin and gestured upward.

They got it, and both used his rock back to leap up and over the other Norruls. The women landed in a hurricane of swords and bullets, taking down the Skulla and shapeshifters, turning mech against mech, and kicking every ass they could find.

Kalan was working them from the other side, and many of the enemy had already turned tail and run.

A blast rocked Valerie and shoved her forward, and her back arched. She was certain her armor was now dented, which would make it hard to heal from whatever had hit her. When she turned she had to roll out of the way of incoming fire as the Bandian, standing atop one of the mechs, continued to shoot at her.

*No more dodging*, she told herself.

No more pain.

No more of this fuckhead Bandian.

With everything she had, she ran at him, but a line of shifters came at her as she did. She *pushed* her fear so they couldn't mend their wounds with their liquid metal or whatever the hell allowed them to heal so fast and cut through them, and then kicked them aside and threw the last. The corpse slammed into the Bandian and knocked him from his mech perch.

A glance showed that Garcia and Flynn had joined the fight, and while two more fighters weren't likely to make or break this battle, the thought of them in action together filled her with excitement.

She sent her sword slashing through the cables that gave power to the mech's legs and after a giant leap she ran up it, shooting at the Bandian as he fled. Nearby shots hit the mech as they aimed for her—just like she'd planned.

The mech started to fall but she hung on, smiling widely.

*"Timber!"* she shouted, leaping free at the last moment. She recovered in time to see the mech slam into the warlord and crush his legs. In two quick strides she had her sword to his throat. "It's over."

Eyes wide, he stared back and nodded. "Over."

"Tell *them!*" she shouted, pulling him out from under the mech and holding his crippled body as a shield and proof that they had won. *"Say* it!"

"It's over!" the Bandian yelled, then hung his head in defeat. Most of the others broke for the tree line, but some knelt in submission.

Kalan remained at the ready as if he didn't believe this

was happening. When he finally relaxed he walked over to Valerie and nodded to Robin, who was keeping an eye on everyone in case they tried anything.

"This is a day for Tol's history books," he stated, nodding appreciatively. "And to think it was because of an outsider."

"But not *only* because of an outsider," she corrected him. "You helped. They all helped."

"Actually, I'm a bit of an outsider too," he corrected, "having been born and raised off-planet."

She tilted her head, considering this. "Wonderful! You can be the Norruls' great hero or leader or whatever, whose coming was foretold."

He looked at her skeptically, then chuckled. "What about him?" he asked, nodding at the Bandian. "He's going to live?"

"We'll hand him over to the locals for punishment," Valerie declared, earning herself an approving grin from the Grayhewn.

They left the death and destruction behind and headed back to the ship. Garcia and Flynn joined them and matched their stride, ready to return to the city and start the long process of getting this place on the right track.

It hadn't been easy so far, but the real challenge was about to begin.

### The *Singlaxian Grandeur*

Kalan stood up as Valerie entered. Bob, Wearl, and Robin were also seated around the table in the aft conference room.

"I just got off the comm with Minister Sslake," Valerie said as she sat. "Poor guy's up to his eyeballs in legal red tape."

"Beats sitting in a prison cell," Robin said dryly.

"Damn right about that," Valerie agreed. "Still, he's got a lot to figure out. Some people are pushing hard for the Damu Michezo to remain open. They're going to be pissed when he shuts it down. Plus, there are still warlords running around out there saying Sslake's not the legitimate leader. It's going to take time for him to get things under control."

"Better him than me," Kalan said.

"On the positive side, he asked me to put him in touch with Colonel Walton."

Robin let out a whistle. "Really? Why?"

"He said he's going to have plenty of jobs that need our particular brand of skills. He wants to see about hiring us, so it looks like we might be sticking around the Vurugu System for a while."

"Wearl likes that idea," Bob reported.

"Yeah, I can hear her, dumbass," Valerie said. She gave the empty seat next to Bob a strange look. She was still getting use to the idea of having an invisible member on the team. She turned to Kalan. "You said there was something you wanted to discuss?"

"There is." He hesitated, not sure where to begin. "When we were on SEDE, my mother gave me a chip. I wasn't able to view what was on it until after we took care of the Bandian, but now I have and, well, it sort of changed my perspective on things."

Valerie tilted her head questioningly. "What was on it?"

"A lot—mostly records, apparently compiled by my father. He was searching for information about my people. There was all sorts of stuff on there, like family trees and ancient journals, as well as my father's personal log."

"Wow," Valerie said. "Pretty cool, but I'm not sure if you needed to call a meeting to discuss that."

Kalan chuckled. "Hang on. There was one piece of information that was particularly interesting. I told you my people were called the *Gah'har'zakanew*. It turns out that was only what the Pallicons called us. We had a different name for ourselves: the Bandians."

Bob's eyes widened. "Wait, what?"

Kalan nodded. "It's true. That ancient race of legendary

warriors? The ones Warlord Nobir named himself after? It turns out I'm one of the last of them."

"Whoa," Robin exclaimed.

"There's a reason so few of us are left. Centuries ago the Pallicons waged war on the Bandians, then hunted us into near extinction. According to my father's records, there's a sect of Pallicons who are *still* dedicated to hunting us. That's why I called this meeting."

Valerie raised an eyebrow. "You want to hire us to take out this sect? No offense, but I don't think you could afford us."

"I *know* I couldn't," Kalan said with a smile. "That's not what I'm asking. Most of my father's records were info on his investigation into where surviving Bandians might be living today. Much of it is rumors and hearsay, but there are a lot of leads he never got the chance to follow up on. He believed our people needed to come together so that we could better protect ourselves."

"Hmm. And you want to carry on his work?"

"I think I have to." He sat up a bit straighter. "Look, I love working with you and I want to keep doing so, but I also have to do this."

Bob rolled his eyes. "Wearl says she's going with you— like there was ever any doubt she'd let you out of her sight."

Kalan waited silently while Valerie thought. He'd never wanted to be on a team as badly as he wanted to be on this one, but at the same time he had a responsibility to carry on his father's work. And the thought of finding other Grayhewns, or rather Bandians? It was enticing.

"Here's what we'll do," Valerie announced. "If we're

going to stay in this system a while, we need to learn more about it. Finding other Grayhewns is as good an excuse as any, so Kalan and Wearl will go off on their search, with the understanding that we'll call them in when we need them. Sort of a reserve unit."

Kalan nodded slowly. "Sounds fair. More than fair, actually."

"One more thing. You're taking Bob with you."

Bob sat up straight as a rod. "Wait, what?"

"The poor guy can't even understand his partner without you," Valerie said to Bob. "We'll see what we can do about that, but in the meantime, he's going to need help. You have a problem going with him?"

Bob thought a moment. "We'd be searching for more Grayhewns, right?"

"Yeah," Kalan confirmed.

"So if we found any females, they'd look like…your mom?"

Robin barked a laugh.

Kalan sighed. "If that's what gets you out the door, sure. Every one of them looks like my mom."

Bob grinned. "When do we leave?"

"It's settled," Valerie said. "You three search for Bandians, but when we call you come running." She paused. "Oh, and one more thing."

She took something off her belt and slid it across the table.

Kalan picked it up, his eyes wide. "A Tralen-14!"

"I got it off one of the Bandian's guards. I heard you liked them."

"Best boss *ever!*" Kalan exclaimed.

"Yeah, well, let's hope you don't have to use it much," she replied. "But I'm fairly certain you will. We've got a lot of work ahead of us."

Robin pointed to the comm screen. "Better get this over with," she suggested.

Valerie opened a comm channel to the *War Axe*.

Colonel Terry Henry Walton leaned back in his chair. Valerie watched him from the screen as she did her best to explain everything that had happened, and would be happening next.

When it was over, he rubbed his chin in thought, then laughed. "You think I'm going to chew your ass because you went off mission, I get that. Maybe I should, but... I had an idea this would happen."

"You had an idea I'd go overboard and incite a coup?"

"It's you, Valerie. From what I hear, it's your thing."

She blushed, not sure whether she should be annoyed or nodding in agreement. Damn, was that really becoming her thing? She let out a laugh, earning her a confused stare from the colonel.

After a moment, he leaned forward as if deciding something. "Thank you for the report. You did what was right by the people of Tol, aliens and natives alike. It's what any decent human being would have done, if they had your abilities. But here's the thing, you need to do what you need to do, and I've spoken with people on our side here... and am thinking you should report directly to Nathan Lowell. I'm going to recommend that next time I talk with him."

Valerie raised one eyebrow. Sergeant Garcia wedged his face into the picture.

"What about me, Colonel? I like being a sergeant, formerly of the FDG, currently of the Bad Company and the Federation's covert missions' team."

"Exactly that, Garcia. The Federation's covert missions' team. Valerie's Elites." His gaze turned back to Valerie. "No one needs to know who you work for, because you don't really work for anyone, do you, Justice Enforcer?"

"I work for those who can't defend themselves," Valerie offered.

"The moral compass guides you. Your gut. Your heart. Whatever you choose. If you need anything, don't hesitate to call. Walton out."

Sergeant Garcia furled his brow. "I feel like I've just been fired."

Valerie smiled, turned, and slapped him on the shoulder hard enough to knock down a normal human. "No, sergeant, you've had the strings cut."

"Strings that didn't do much to control you," he replied with a laugh.

She leaned back, stretching her arms behind her head, and smiled. "A weight has been lifted from my shoulders, a weight I didn't know I was carrying. I feel like I could take on another world, maybe two or three."

Robin groaned behind her. "Just when I thought we might have a chance at reigning you in."

"Ha! As if that will ever be possible."

"So… it's business as usual?" Garcia asked. "I mean, just to be clear… what next?"

"We keep on, keeping on with Terry and his people as allies as we continue to export justice to all the jackoffs out here who need it. Let's get to it, people. This was just the beginning."

*FINIS*

Many of you reading this have read my Reclaiming Honor series with Michael Anderle, and are therefore familiar with Valerie and Robin. Thank you so very much for sticking with me all this time--eight books in that series, and now we have this series starting! Can you believe it has already come about? It was less than a year ago that Michael and I started this little adventure.

And now we've wrapped PT into it. If you didn't know, PT and I have worked together before. That time, it was a children's series and therefore very different (under a penance). I think what happened was he mentioned me in one of his Youtube videos, I checked out his books and loved them, and then we started chatting and decided to try and work on something. If you haven't read his fantasy books (the Zane Halloway series) you are missing out. Working with him on our children's books was a dream, so when I started working with Michael I promptly told him we needed PT as a collaborator. He agreed, and PT and I both wrote (separate) books in the Age of Magic Kurtherian Gambit spinoff. Those were fun, and our books had some crossover, so we decided to give this Age of Expansion writing a try--and I'm so glad we did! Hopefully you agree that the outcome was better than either of us would have produced on our own.

Coming at it from reading any of our previous works must be an interesting experience, and we would love to hear your thoughts. Join us on Facebook, where we're often discussing our works with fans (and sometimes haters, lol).

There are others of you who have never read anything by us before this book. I find it fascinating that the reading experience will be so completely different from the rest. Do the characters feel fleshed out to the same degree? Does their backstory feel like it makes you curious to go off and read those other books? What do you think about the slightly different styles of writing between us? Again, we'd love to discuss all of this and more.

What's next? Well, we have more books in this series, naturally, and they should be coming at you fairly fast. You should also, of course, read all of our other books and the other books in the Age of Expansion. Oh man, you have a lot of reading ahead of you! Good thing you love books, right?

On the non-KGU side, I have my Seppukarian Universe that I've been building up with several co-writers. Within this, Jonathan Yanez and I did a series called War Wolves, which has been high on the charts since it launched. I have my Shadow Corps books, which are basically science fantasy (science fiction with magic). And Podium is producing audiobooks for both of those series, as well as the one that started off the Seppukarian Universe, the Syndicate Wars books. Podium was the group behind The Martian, to give you an idea of how cool this is. We are excited, and have such narrators as Allyson Johnson reading the books--she did the Honor Harrington series by David Weber, so we're standing among giants.

I hope you'll continue down the Valerie's Elites series, and stick with me as a reader for years to come. I have BIG plans. As an author I went full-time about six months before writing this book, and therefore have time to actually write the books I want to write. Thanks to you all, I can actually pay rent and feed my children while living the dream! Being full-time means I don't have to stay up until two in the morning to get my writing in after working to make someone else rich. It means I can get rest, and not have a line of ZZzzzzzZZZZzzz across my pages from nodding off all the time while writing. Believe me, my editors love it! They used to ask me things about some of my stories, and I had been so tired when writing, I couldn't even remember what they were talking about! I feel so blessed that those days are gone, and because of that I'm going to write my heart out, put my all into these books for you all, and never stop.

Join me for the ride!

## AUTHOR NOTES - PT HYLTON

WRITTEN DECEMBER 3RD, 2017

A big "thank you" to all of you for reading this book.

I've known Justin for about a year and a half. Our friendship started not because we are both writers, but because we both have YouTube channels where we talk about books and writing. I stumbled upon one of his videos, enjoyed it, and mentioned him in one of my videos. He caught that video and dropped me a note. Now we're writing awesome sci-fi books together.

What I'm saying is the Internet is a weird place.

Here's another example: an hour ago, I was in the backyard with my daughter, looking through her telescope at the super moon. Then I came inside and wrote a battle scene on a moon where... Well, you'll find out in book 2.

Okay, time for some thank yous:

Thanks to Michael for letting us play in this amazing toybox he's built.

Thanks for Justin for inviting me to write with him and sharing these characters he's spent nine books developing.

Thanks to Craig for shepherding the Age of Expansion.

Thanks to Lynne for editing prowess and Steve for organizational super heroics.

And thanks once again to you for reading.

If you want to check out my other stuff, here's a ten-second pitch:

**Storm Raiders** (Age of Magic) – In a future where Etheric technology is mistaken for magic, a young woman fights for justice among a Viking-esque culture that can control the weather. This series has some cool Valerie tie-ins… and I have one *really* big tie-in planned for book five.

**The Savage Earth** – In a future where the Earth has been overrun by feral vampires, the last remnant of humanity survives by continually circumnavigating the globe in an airship, always staying in the daylight. But when the ship malfunctions, they're all in big trouble, and it's a race against the clock to fix the ship or be forced to survive the night on the surface.

As Justin mentioned in his author note, we have big plans for this series. I can't wait to hear your thoughts on this book. It's going to get wild!

Happy reading,
PT

## AUTHOR NOTES - MICHAEL ANDERLE

WRITTEN DECEMBER 6, 2017

Hello!

First, let me thank you for not only reading the story but also Justin and PT's author notes and now to my own, as well!

As the creator of the Kurtherian Gambit Universe, I always enjoy learning what each new collaborator wants to write into the universe based and their interests and how they 'found' both the Kurtherian Gambit, or me, or other collaborators.

I am celebrating one full year of collaborating with Justin Sloan on December 8th with his Reclaiming Honor Books. It seems so very long ago (way more than a year) that we put that book up for pre-order and knocked it out of the park with 2,400 pre-orders in three weeks.

Then, I almost freaked out when the final update for the book (which must be done 72 hours before release) WOULDN'T UPDATE!

If we had failed to get the update online, then all 2,400 of the readers would receive the WRONG book.

OH CRAP!

I was told on a back channel how I could get ahold of someone with some clout at Amazon and I admit, I wasn't shy with trying to throw around ANY success I had to get the update fixed in time. I have heard HORROR stories of authors whose pre-orders were sent out incorrectly.

You RARELY ever get past that screwup.

I know of one very successful author whose book's reviews are around a 3 star because of a messed-up pre-order.

I shiver right now thinking about it.

Anyway, I was contacted and the file (it was their fault) was fixed in time. Crises averted.

When the Age of Magic started up, Justin was right there pimping PT and we are HAPPY he joined us. His stories in the Age of Magic (Storms of Magic) are just a blast. Personally, we are going to have to change his covers, or do something as they don't convey the magic that is in the stories, and I think that is causing us issues on the sales side of his books.

Which sucks, because they are a lot of fun to read with characters and descriptions which make you go 'inside' the stories.

If you get a chance, visit either Justin's or PT's author pages and check out their books, I'll put links below for the items I've mentioned above.

Ad Aeternitatem,
Michael

Reclaiming Honor Series:
http://books2read.com/ReclaimingHonor
Storms of Magic Series:
http://books2read.com/StormsOfMagic
Justin Sloan Website: http://www.justinsloanauthor.com/
PT Hylton's Website: http://www.pthylton.com/

## ~SEPPUKARIAN UNIVERSE~

(Space Opera Fantasy)

### SHADOW CORPS

Shadow Corps (01) - Shadow Worlds (02) - Shadow Fleet (03)

### WAR WOLVES

Bring the Thunder (01) - Click Click Boom (02) -
Light Em Up (03)

## ~SEPPUKARIAN UNIVERSE~

(Space Marines and Time Travel )

### SYNDICATE WARS

First Strike (01) - The Resistance (02) - Fault Line (03) -
False Dawn (04) - Empire Rising (05)

## FANTASY

### FALLS OF REDEMPTION

(Epic Fantasy Series)
Land of Gods (01) - Retribution Calls (02) -
Tears of Devotion (03)

## MODERN NECROMANCY

(Supernatural Thriller)

Death Marked (01) - Death Bound (02) - Death Crowned (03)

## CURSED NIGHT

(Supernatural Thriller with Werewolves and Vampires)

Hounds of God (01) - Hounds of Light (02) -

*Coming in 2018* Hounds of Blood (03)

## ALLIE STROM

(MG Urban Fantasy Trilogy)

Allie Strom and the Ring of Solomon (01)

Allie Strom and the Sword of the Spirit (02)

Allie Strom and the Tenth Worthy (03)

## THE BORIS CHRONICLES
### * with Paul C. Middleton *

Evacuation (1) - Retaliation (2) - Revelations (3) -
Redemption (04) *Coming soon*

## RECLAIMING HONOR
### * with Justin Sloan *

Justice Is Calling (01) - Claimed By Honor (02) -
Judgement Has Fallen (03) - Angel of Reckoning (04) -
Born Into Flames (05) - Defending The Lost (06) -
Saved By Valor (07) - Return of Victory (08)

## THE ETHERIC ACADEMY
### * with TS PAUL *

Alpha Class (01) - ALPHA CLASS - Engineering (02)

## TERRY HENRY "TH" WALTON CHRONICLES
### * with Craig Martelle *

Nomad Found (01) - Nomad Redeemed (02) -
Nomad Unleashed (03) - Nomad Supreme (04) -
Nomad's Fury (05) - Nomad's Justice (06) -
Nomad Avenged (07) - Nomad Mortis (08) - Nomad's Force (09)
Nomad's Galaxy (10)

## TRIALS AND TRIBULATIONS
### * with Natalie Grey *
Risk Be Damned (01) - Damned to Hell (02)

## ~THE AGE OF MAGIC~

## THE RISE OF MAGIC
### * with CM Raymond and LE Barbant *
Restriction (01) - Reawakening (02) - Rebellion (03) - Revolution (04) - Unlawful Passage (05) - Darkness Rises (06) - The Gods Beneath (07) - Reborn (08)

## THE HIDDEN MAGIC CHRONICLES
### * with Justin Sloan *
Shades of Light (01) - Shades of Dark (02) - Shades of Glory (03) - Shades of Justice (04)

## STORMS OF MAGIC
### * with PT Hylton *
Storm Raiders (01) - Storm Callers (02) - Storm Breakers (03) - Storm Warrior (04)

## TALES OF THE FEISTY DRUID
### * with Candy Crum *
The Arcadian Druid (01) - The Undying Illusionist (02) - The Frozen Wasteland (03) - The Deceiver (04) - The Lost (05) - The Damned (06)

## PATH OF HEROES
### * with Brandon Barr *
Rogue Mage (01)

## A NEW DAWN
### * with Amy Hopkins *
Dawn of Destiny (01) - Dawn of Darkness (02) -
Dawn of Deliverance (03) - Dawn of Days (04)

## ~THE AGE OF EXPANSION~

## THE ASCENSION MYTH
### * with Ell Leigh Clarke *
Awakened (01) - Activated (02) - Called (03) - Sanctioned (04) -
Rebirth (05) - Retribution (06) - Cloaked (07) -
Bourne (08)

## CONFESSIONS OF A SPACE ANTHROPOLOGIST
### * with Ell Leigh Clarke *
Giles Kurns: Rogue Operator (01)

## THE UPRISE SAGE
### * with Amy Duboff *
Covert Talents (01) - Endless Advance (02) - Veiled Designs (03)

## BAD COMPANY
### * with Craig Martelle *
The Bad Company (01) - Blockade (02)

## SHORT STORIES

*You Don't Touch John's Cousin*

Frank Kurns Stories of the UnknownWorld 01 (7.5)

*Bitch's Night Out*

Frank Kurns Stories of the UnknownWorld 02 (9.5)

**\* With Natalie Grey \***

*Bellatrix*

Frank Kurns Stories of the Unknownworld 03 (13.25)

## AUDIOBOOKS

*Available at Amazon, Audible.com and iTunes*